The Instant Marco Set Eyes On The Woman, Every Thought Vanished From His Head, Replaced By A Whispered Demand Unlike Any He'd Ever Heard Before.

Take this woman. Possess her. Make her yours.

Without hesitation, he approached her, compelled to obey. She stood in the three-story entryway of the office building, absorbing the elegant décor. Sunlight streamed through the tinted windows, capturing her in its golden embrace. It plunged into hair of so deep an ebony that it rivaled the nighttime sky, even as it turned her complexion to pure cream. It took every ounce of self-control Marco had to keep from sweeping her into his arms and carrying her off.

God help him, but he *wanted* her....

Dear Reader,

Have you ever been desperate? I mean truly desperate. Your heart's desire hovers in front of you, bright and shiny and tantalizing. But you can't reach it because your path is blocked by seemingly insurmountable obstacles. What do you do? Do you give up...or do you try every means at your disposal to attain your dream?

Most of us have experienced that situation at some point in our lives. I have with my career, and in my personal life. I wanted to be a writer more than anything, and I was willing to do whatever it took to accomplish my goal. There were endless obstacles, but I didn't care. None seemed impossible to overcome—at least, not to me. One of my happiest days was when I finally attained my dream, and received that incredible call from my brand-new editor, telling me I'd sold my first book.

In *Dante's Stolen Wife,* Marco Dante experiences that desperate desire, only it's for a woman—a woman who belongs to his twin brother. And Marco will overcome any obstacles, do whatever it takes, to have the woman he loves. This is one of my favorite stories ever. I love the idea of a man pushed to the limit. A man forced to make outrageous choices and then deal with the consequences of his actions. And I love writing about a man who will risk all to win the love of his soul mate.

So what obstacles stand in your way...and what are you willing to do to overcome them and attain your heart's desire? Will you give up? Or will you fight...and win?

Here's to your success,

Day Leclaire

DAY LECLAIRE

DANTE'S STOLEN WIFE

Silhouette® Desire

Published by Silhouette Books

America's Publisher of Contemporary Romance

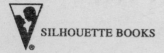

SILHOUETTE BOOKS

ISBN-13: 978-0-373-76870-7
ISBN-10:   0-373-76870-2

DANTE'S STOLEN WIFE

DAY LECLAIRE

USA TODAY bestselling author Day Leclaire lives and works in the perfect setting—on an island off the North Carolina coast. Living in an environment where she can connect with primal elements that meld the moodiness of an ever-changing ocean, unfettered wetlands teeming with every creature imaginable, and the ferocity of both hurricanes and nor'easters that batter the fragile island, she's discovered the perfect setting for writing passionate books that offer a unique combination of humor, emotion and unforgettable characters.

Described by Harlequin Books as "one of our most popular writers ever!" Day's tremendous worldwide popularity has made her a member of Harlequin's prestigious Five Star Club, with sales totaling more than five million books. She is a three-time winner of both the Colorado Award of Excellence and the Golden Quill Award. She's won Romantic Times BOOKreviews Career Achievement and Love and Laughter awards, the Holt Medallion, a Booksellers Best Award and has received an impressive ten nominations for the prestigious Romance Writers of America RITA® Award.

Day's romances touch the heart and make you care about her characters as much as she does. In Day's own words, "I adore writing romances, and can't think of a better way to spend each day." For more information, visit Day on her Web site at www.dayleclaire.com.

To Danielle Andre,
who knows all about chasing her dreams.

One

"I'm warning you, Marco. No more scandals. If your family continues to be featured in the gossip magazines, we will have no choice but to place our account elsewhere. The reports have carried all the way to Italy. I even caught Ariana reading them. My own daughter!"

Marco Dante inclined his head. "I understand, Vittorio. We don't know why *The Snitch* has embarked on this campaign against Dantes. But I promise you, I plan to put an end to it, no matter what it takes. You and my father were good friends. We appreciated your business when he ran our jewelry business, and now that we're moving back into the European market, we hope to have your patronage once again."

Vittorio gave an expressive shrug to accompany his expression of vague regret. "I'd enjoy seeing the names of Dante and Romano mated once more. But we're extremely private people. We choose our associates with great care." He deliberately switched to Italian to add weight to his words. "If you wish to have our support for your European expansion, you must take care of this problem."

Marco nodded. Unfortunately, they'd lost the Romanos' backing years ago, shortly after his father's death. At that time, Dantes teetered on the brink of ruin, and would have gone under if not for Marco's brother, Severo, who'd assumed the reins of the family jewelry empire straight out of college. During his first year on the job, he'd been forced to scale back on the size of the business, stripping Dantes to the bone.

Little by little over the past decade, under Sev's brilliant direction, Dantes had made an impressive resurrection and now stood on the verge of regaining their place as the premier jewelers, worldwide. At least they would if they recovered the European trade they'd lost. And Marco planned to make certain that happened.

It was imperative to their success that they return the Romanos to the fold, something he'd worked tirelessly on for the past year. And it was all due to a single ancient expression, one that had floated around the most elite circles for countless generations—*Where the Romanos lead, Europe follows.* The Romanos were considered Italian royalty and Marco intended to have Europe follow Vittorio and Ariana straight to Dantes' front door. And now that possibility hovered within reach.

The Romanos craved the glorious designs Dantes offered, designs that featured only the finest stones available, including the fire diamonds that could be found nowhere else in the world other than in one of Dantes' display cases. But the Romanos wanted them without any unsavory scandal attached. Thanks to the type of gossip *The Snitch* liked to dish on a weekly basis—as well as their current focus on the four Dante brothers—Marco had reached an impasse with Vittorio Romano.

It was an impasse Marco planned to overcome, no matter what it took. He clapped Vittorio on the shoulder. "Consider it done. We'll deal with *The Snitch,* after which we look forward to providing for your every need." He held out his hand. "Thank you for coming all the way to San Francisco. I'm sorry Ariana didn't accompany you on this trip. My family would have enjoyed meeting her."

Vittorio grinned. "She is lovely, my Ariana, is she not?" He returned Marco's handshake. "Next time I am in San Francisco I will insist she come with me."

"We'll make it a family affair."

"*Eccellente.* I look forward to it. I understand Severo just became engaged to that new designer you recently acquired. Francesca Sommers? Please offer the couple my warmest congratulations."

With that, Vittorio walked briskly toward the huge etched glass doors that graced the entryway of the Dantes San Francisco offices, and held one open for a woman entering the building. He offered her a courtly nod and a smile of pure masculine appreciation, before exiting. Not that Marco noticed Vittorio's departure. The instant he set eyes on the woman, he paused, riveted. Every thought vanished from his head, replaced by a whispered demand unlike any he'd ever experienced before.

Take this woman. Possess her. Make her yours.

Without hesitation, he approached, compelled to obey. She stood in the three-story entryway, absorbing the elegant decor. Sunlight streamed through the tinted windows, capturing her within its golden embrace. It plunged into hair so deep an ebony that it rivaled the nighttime sky, while turning her complexion to pure cream. She tipped her head back to look at the glass sculpture hanging above the receptionist's desk, a sculpture that resembled leaping flames, and her hair sheeted down her back in heavy waves. It took every ounce of self-control Marco possessed to keep from sweeping her into his arms and carrying her off.

She walked up to the receptionist and he caught the murmur of her voice asking for information. The man behind the desk glanced at Marco, frowned in momentary confusion—no doubt trying to decide which twin he was, something that amused Marco no end—then pointed in his direction. With a nod of thanks, the woman approached and Marco smiled in open delight. At his smile, the receptionist made a frantic effort to catch the woman's attention, before giving up with a shrug.

Marco only had eyes for the woman. God help him, but he wanted her. It was as though someone had delved deep into his mind and plucked loose his personal image of perfection, then created this glorious example of femininity from that image. She stood at the exact right kissing height, not too short, nor too tall, with a full, smiling mouth he couldn't wait to explore. Her features were delicate and ivory pale, with a straight, no-nonsense nose, determined jawline and high, arching cheekbones that lifted her from beauty to sheer poetry.

His gaze dipped lower and his forward momentum faltered. She was dressed for business, but no fabric existed that could conceal a body created for the pleasures of the night. Full breasts strained against her crisp, tailored navy suit, and some kind soul had designed the jacket so that it nipped in at a waist he could have spanned with two hands before flirting with the curves below— tight round curves that were the devil's own temptation.

He must have made some sound—a groan, if he were a betting man—because she studied him curiously. Her eyes were a deep teal blue and made a striking contrast to her dark hair. Before he could introduce himself, she stuck out her hand. "Ah, Mr. Dante," she said. "Just the man I was looking for. It's a pleasure to finally meet you. I'm Caitlyn Vaughn."

She said it as though he should recognize her name, but he couldn't recall ever having heard of her before, maybe because in the last sixty seconds every single one of his brain cells had leaked out of his ears. Not that he'd admit his foolishness. "Of course," he said with his most charming smile. "It's a pleasure to meet you, as well."

He took the hand she offered, and that's when it happened. A hard jolt of electricity zapped him, sinking deep into muscle and bone. He'd never felt anything like it. It didn't hurt, precisely, just surprised and shocked. Based on Caitlyn's startled expression and the way she jerked free of his hold, she must have felt it, as well... and didn't like it.

"Oh! What was that?" she asked.

"I'm not certain."

But he suspected he knew. Based on his reaction toward Caitlyn, as well as what his eldest brother, Sev, had described, this must be The Inferno. Such an odd Dante blessing—or was it a curse?—that irrevocably bound the men in his family with their true soul mates, the one and only woman they would ever love. Marco and his brothers had believed the story to be a charming family fairy tale. But ever since Sev had encountered the unremitting burn of its existence, Marco wondered if he would experience it. Wondered if he were capable of experiencing it.

He was a man who adored women. All women. He loved everything about them. The unending glorious shapes and sizes. The delightful palate of hues. The music of feminine voices. Their unique scent. As far as he was concerned, women were as beautiful as they were fascinating and he delighted in each and every one. The idea of choosing one specific flower, instead of the bounty nature offered struck him as unreasonable. And yet...

When he looked at Caitlyn, he saw a woman who was a bounty in and of herself, a bouquet of such depth and beauty that it would take the rest of his life to fully explore each and every aspect. Where hardheaded Sev fought, where the accountant soul in his twin brother Lazzaro questioned and analyzed, where problemsolver Nicolò flat-out denied, the romantic in Marco accepted. He'd take this gift from the gods.

"I've been waiting for you," he told her.

* * *

He'd been waiting for her? Caitlyn stared at Lazzaro Dante as though hypnotized, struggling to get some part of her, any part of her, functioning again after that peculiar handshake and her even more peculiar reaction to it.

During her job interview to be the new head of finance for the national branch of Dantes, Lazz had been pointed out to her. He was in charge of the international end of the business, a far larger, more complicated department. And though she wouldn't work directly with him, they would come into regular contact during the course of their workday. She'd been told she'd be introduced to him directly after she arrived at Dantes, but it never occurred to her that he'd be waiting for her in the lobby, until the receptionist had pointed him out.

"It really is kind of you to meet me here on my first day, Mr. Dante, but—" The shock she experienced when they first shook hands continued to tickle her palm and she rubbed her thumb across it. To her amusement he copied the gesture, distracting her. "Okay, I have to know. What was that?"

He eyed her sympathetically. "Did I hurt you, *cara?* I am sorry."

"Hurt me? Oh, no…not really." That surprised her, given the intensity of the shock. "It was just…unexpected."

Worse, though it seemed a ridiculous concept, that shock seemed to have intensified her awareness of him. When she'd first seen him last week after her final interview, she'd have described Lazz as incredibly attractive, almost too good-looking for a woman's peace of mind. But now… A slight panic stole over her. Somehow, with that single touch, she became keenly aware of him and the startling congruity that formed between them. It felt as though a light switch had been flipped, igniting thoughts and emotions she'd never experienced before. She didn't understand it, didn't want to understand it.

In all her twenty-eight years, she'd never done anything to jeopardize her professional career. How many times had Gran warned her about that? How many times had her grandmother used her own life as a hard-won lesson? Caitlyn understood the cardinal rules, had learned them well. Don't let a man charm you into ruining your career for a brief ride over the rainbow. Because all that waited on the other side was fool's gold. And build a strong foundation with a serious-minded man capable of staying power, who believed in the same things you did. Well, she'd listened and learned. She wouldn't allow any man to take her for a ride. And yet…

Their surroundings seemed to melt away, and the noises faded to a soft murmur. The light appeared to dim until only the two of them were caught within the sun's halo. Every beat of her heart sent desire coursing deeper and more powerfully through her veins until the sheer want of him overrode every other thought and emotion.

"Caitlyn," he murmured.

Her name on his tongue made her think of wine and poetry, and though he didn't have an accent, his voice contained a noticeable Mediterranean lilt, deep and ripe and musical. He held out his hand and almost—*almost*—she took it, willing to follow wherever he led and tumble into bliss with him wherever and whenever he suggested, even right here and right now.

Instead she used whatever final scrap of common sense she still possessed and made a production of checking her watch. "I'm due in personnel in five minutes." Instinctively she moved to extend her hand again in a businesslike parting, but withdrew it quickly, and took several steps toward the elevator. Some irresistible compulsion had her turn and offer a final nod of farewell. "I'll see you soon, Mr. Dante. I believe we have an appointment scheduled for ten."

At that, a blinding smile lit his face. "I didn't realize. My assistant neglected to mention it." He advanced in her direction. "But, why wait? Why not move our appointment forward?"

The elevator doors opened just then and she didn't dare linger or she'd cave to his request. Heaven only knew what would happen between them if she did. Good Lord! On her first day of work, no less. "Ten o'clock," she repeated. "I look forward to seeing you then."

She darted inside the car, fighting to maintain a calm expression while the doors whisked silently closed. To her relief Lazz didn't give chase but stood perfectly still, his features carved into lines of determination as he watched her retreat. Because that's what it was, a full-scale, tail-turning, white-flag-flying, unabashed retreat.

The instant the doors shut, she leaned against the

back wall and closed her eyes. She hadn't been in the building for a full thirty seconds and look at how much she'd already risked as a result of a single, casual handshake. What in the world had gotten into her? For that matter, what had gotten into Lazzaro Dante? Whatever had just happened between them, from this minute on, she needed to put such foolishness aside and focus on work.

Thirty minutes later, she realized that not only couldn't she forget, but it had become an absolute impossibility. Something about that single touch had changed her. Caitlyn struggled to concentrate on the reams of HR paperwork to be filled out and the workaday tour of facilities, trying to convince herself that vital information was being given. But with every minute that passed, she grew more and more tense, knowing she'd soon see Lazz and find out if she'd imagined her reaction to him.

When the moment finally arrived, she greeted him with a professional demeanor, meant to conceal her nervousness. "So, we meet again." She caught the faintest hitch in his step and a tiny frown formed between his hazel eyes before he held out his hand, a hand she eyed with undisguised apprehension. "That's brave of you, after what happened last time. But if you're game, so am I."

He paused a beat before inclining his head. "I'm willing."

To her relief she didn't receive a zap again. And then the relief faded to a vague disappointment. Maybe she'd imagined that surge of electricity. And though she felt an unmistakable warmth toward the man holding her hand, it bore little resemblance to the unrelenting desire she'd felt just a scant hour before. Not that she let on.

Lazz studied her with just as much interest as earlier, and the hungry spark in her eyes remained, as well. "Welcome to Dantes. I'm looking forward to getting to know you better," he said.

As before, there was no misinterpreting the intent behind his comment. It was an invitation, Caitlyn realized in that instant. Right now the two of them teetered on the verge of a relationship that went beyond business. She was intrigued by the power it offered. Her move. She could either back away and put an end to it. Or she could take the next step—cautiously, of course—and see where it led. Time seemed to slow, giving her a moment to consider

She couldn't be certain that what she'd experienced in the lobby of Dantes had anything to do with love, but she would never have gotten as far as she had in business if she shied away from a challenge out of sheer timidity or contrariness. The opportunity in front of her was certainly a challenge, but she also spied all the pieces necessary to build the foundation her grandmother had so often talked about. He was sexy and successful, but most of all smart. Someone she could build a castle with. And the tingle they'd shared earlier? Lucky bonus.

She didn't hesitate another instant. She offered Lazz a brilliant smile and surrendered to whatever fate ordained. Maybe their current setting had put a slight damper on that sizzle of attraction. She'd just have to wait and see what happened from here. The bottom line was…whatever had occurred in the lobby of Dantes, she wanted more.

"I'm really looking forward to getting to know you," she said.

Two

Six Weeks Later

Caitlyn took her customary seat around a generous-size smoked glass table, joining the two women with whom she'd formed a fast friendship over the six weeks she'd been working at Dantes. They always met for lunch at the same time and place thanks to Lazz, who'd been generous enough to offer the use of a small conference room connected to his office.

The minute they were seated, Britt preened for them, showing off a stunning pair of diamond earrings. "Check these out. They're a Dantes exclusive. Aren't they gorgeous?"

"Who gave those to you and how do I meet someone like that," Angie demanded.

"I bought them for myself," Britt confessed with a hint of bravado. "I figured it was the only way I'd ever get a pair."

"On whose salary?" When Britt simply made a face, Angie let it go and glanced at them with barely suppressed excitement. "Well, I have news. You won't believe what I heard." She spared a brief glance toward the door exiting onto the executive floor to confirm they'd shut it before staring uneasily at the open doorway leading to Lazz's office, a doorway only steps from their table. "Maybe I shouldn't say anything here."

"Lazz is out to lunch with his brother, Nicolò, if that's what you're worried about. I booked the reservation myself," Britt reassured. "No one can overhear us."

"Okay." Even so, she lowered her voice. "I heard something interesting at Dantes Exclusive."

Caitlyn understood that to mean Dantes' private retail operation, a select by-invitation-only showroom that catered to the elite. Angie had started there as a saleswoman two full decades ago, before climbing steadily up the retail end of the corporate ladder.

"Who visited this time?" Caitlyn asked. She'd forgotten to leave her reading glasses in her office—an all-too-common occurrence—and shoved them into her hair on top of her head. "Show business, finance or royalty?"

Britt offered a catlike grin. "I'll bet I know."

Angie laughed. "Since you're his personal assistant, I'll bet you do, too."

Caitlyn blinked in surprise. "Are you talking about Lazz?" At Angie's nod of confirmation, Caitlyn wrinkled her brow in confusion and asked, "Why is it so odd that he'd be at Exclusive?"

Angie paused, before dropping her next bombshell. "Maybe because he was looking at engagement rings."

Both women gazed at Caitlyn with broad smiles, while she sat for a long moment in stunned silence, rubbing her palm. "No. You can't really think…"

"Not only do I think. I'll bet dinner at Le Premier on it."

"Well, it makes perfect sense to me," Britt offered. "You two hit it off right from the start. Plus you're so much alike. You're both practical. Logical. Not to mention financial geniuses. It takes every bit of my ability to keep up with him. But the two of you… Whenever you're together, it's like you're talking in shorthand. It's almost as if you're already an old married couple."

Angie made a face. "You make it sound so dull. It isn't like that, is it, Caitlyn?" A frown of distress touched her brow. "I mean, there's romance, right? Excitement? Give an old woman hope. Tell me there's romance and excitement, even if it's a lie."

Caitlyn felt herself blushing. "Of course there's romance and excitement," she muttered. Somewhere.

"Now if it were Marco," Britt offered, "I guarantee there'd never be a dull moment. Have you crossed paths with him yet?" Before Caitlyn could respond, she gave an impatient click of her tongue. "No, of course you wouldn't have. He just flew in from overseas today. I think he's only been home two other times. Once was about a month ago when Sev threw a bash for Francesca to publicize the release of the Dante's Heart Collection."

"I was in New York at the time," Caitlyn reminded her.

"Oh, right. And then Marco showed up for Sev's wedding."

Caitlyn shook her head. "New York, again. I did meet Sev last week, though," she said. But for some reason, Lazz had shown a notable reluctance to introduce her to the various members of the Dante clan, something that filled her with a vague unease. "But he's the only other Dante so far."

Britt tilted her head to one side. "Hmm. Sounds to me like Lazz wants to keep you all to himself. He's probably afraid that if he introduces you to his brothers, you'll decide you like one of them better, especially his tw—"

"Don't be ridiculous," Caitlyn interrupted, taking instant exception. "I was attracted to Lazz from the minute we first shook hands." Just because the weeks since hadn't lived up to that initial contact didn't mean that bone-deep attraction didn't still exist. "As for his brothers, I expect I'll meet them at his grandparents' anniversary party tonight."

"Nothing against Lazz, but..." Britt leaned back in her chair, a dreamy expression slipping across her face. "Don't you just once long to have Zorro come sweeping down and carry you off?"

"And have his wicked way with you?" added Angie.

"Instead of planning every move down to the last nanosecond?" Britt's gaze sharpened on Caitlyn, filled with open curiosity. "Is that how he makes love?" After an instant of stunned silence, she added with a mischievous smile, "Oh, come on, Angie. Back me up here. It's not like you haven't been wondering the same thing. I just want to know if Lazz makes love the same way he works. Is it by the numbers, or is he a bit more creative in the sack?"

"Britt Jones!"

She must have realized she'd gone too far. She mouthed a hasty apology to Caitlyn before deliberately changing the subject, asking a question about Dantes' new retail collection—Dante's Heart—which had been launched five short weeks ago, right before Sev Dante's marriage to designer, Francesca Sommers.

Caitlyn studied her friends uneasily as they chatted about the whirlwind marriage of the eldest of the four Dante brothers. To tell the truth, she couldn't have answered Britt's impertinent question even if she'd been so inclined. She didn't have a clue how Lazz made love, since matters hadn't progressed quite that far. Though now that she thought about it, *why* hadn't they had sex?

Because they were busy putting all the pieces together, that's why. Well, clearly not *all* the pieces. She wanted to be sure they were standing on firm ground before taking the next step. And although that sounded good in theory, it still didn't answer the question to her satisfaction.

She pretended to give her full attention to her lunch as she considered the matter. It seemed that after the sizzle and heat of her first meeting with Lazz in the lobby of Dantes, the sexual tension between them had eased to a pleasant, comfortable warmth. Since that first shocking handshake, she'd never again experienced the spark and burn, no matter how many times they touched or kissed, nor how often she longed for it to happen just once more, if only so she'd know she hadn't imagined it.

Their dates had been enjoyable. No. That struck her as too bland a description for her time with Lazz. They felt passion. Sure they did. Lazz left no doubt as to his feelings for her. He'd made it crystal clear how much he wanted her, and expressed his impatience to take their relationship to the next step. If anything, she had slowed the pace, something he'd reluctantly allowed. She picked at her salad. And why had she done that?

She released her breath in a slow sigh. Because she'd been waiting. Waiting to feel that amazing rush of emotion again. To be swept away just as Angie described. But with each passing day, it became clearer and clearer that she and Lazz were as alike as two peas in a pod, both far too practical for their own good.

It looked as if all the pieces for a proper foundation were there, just the way Gran had instructed, but as she and Lazz worked at putting those pieces in place, she realized some vital parts were missing. Such a shame since she really, truly liked Lazz. And too bad that whatever spark had first ignited between them had died in the weeks since to no more than a warm glow.

She set her fork down and slipped her glasses onto the tip of her nose, her "getting down to business" mode. It was time to face facts. She wanted more than a warm glow. She wanted what she'd felt when she and Lazz had first met. Tonight she intended to confront Lazz, to take their relationship to the next step and discover once and for all whether the spark still existed, waiting to be fanned to life, or if it had been extinguished before it ever had a chance to catch fire.

"Caitlyn?"

Her head jerked upward and she realized her friends were standing by the door leading into the hallway, staring at her in concern. "You okay?" Britt prompted. "What are you waiting for?"

Caitlyn knew what she was waiting for, what she wanted and who she intended to have. "Zorro," she murmured in reply. "I'm waiting for Zorro."

"No, Marco." His grandmother's whispered order stopped him in his tracks, preventing him from bursting from Lazz's office into the conference room and confronting the women they'd just overheard. "You cannot go in there. You would embarrass them."

He hesitated, driven by a compulsion so strong he shook with the effort to control it. "Don't try and stop me, Nonna. I'm going to put an end to this. I've waited so long to return home again, to have an opportunity to finally approach Caitlyn. These past few weeks have nearly driven me insane. And now…" He shook his head. "I can't let Lazz propose to her. She doesn't belong to him."

His grandmother crossed to his side and slid a gentle hand along the clenched muscles of his arm. "He claims otherwise, *nipote*. You have been gone much of this past month and a half. A lot has happened in that short period of time. Lazzaro and Caitlyn Vaughn have experienced The Inferno."

He spoke between clenched teeth. "That's not possible."

"Of course it is. Just because you are attracted to this woman—"

"No. You don't understand." Marco swiveled to face his grandmother, barely able to restrain himself. "Caitlyn and *I* experienced The Inferno, not Lazz. And he knew it. That's why he sent me away, Nonna. Deliberately. He found crisis after crisis in the foreign offices that required my personal attention. The few times I've been home, Caitlyn has conveniently been sent off on Dantes business. And it was all done to keep me away from her so Lazz could take her for himself. Something his assistant, Britt, said to me on the phone the other day finally clued me in on what he's been up to."

Nonna stared at him, shocked. "Do you realize what you are suggesting?"

He held out his right hand, palm up, and dug his thumb into the center where the bond had first formed. He softened his voice so they wouldn't be overheard. "I felt the burn the day Caitlyn arrived at Dantes. From the moment I saw her, I suspected. But when I touched her, I knew. It was her first day at work, her first few minutes under our roof. We met in the lobby and shook hands and ever since that moment the need for her has grown. Grown to unbearable levels. I realize now that she mistook me for Lazz." His expression darkened. "And that when my dear brother discovered that fact, he took great care not to correct her error."

"She does not know you are twins?"

"Apparently not."

Nonna sank into the chair in front of Lazz's desk and

made the sign of the cross. "You came here to confront him over this, to demand he give her up, didn't you?"

"I landed an hour ago and came to find him," he confirmed. "I want to know why he's trying to take my woman."

"From what Lazz said, we all thought—" She broke off with a look of confusion. "We assumed he'd felt The Inferno for Caitlyn."

"You assumed wrong." Marco hesitated, a sudden thought occurring to him. "Or did you? Is it possible that twins can feel The Inferno for the same woman?"

To his relief, she didn't hesitate. "No, Marco. That much I do know." She made a helpless gesture. "What I do not understand is why he would claim her if she is not his. How could he make such a mistake?"

"I haven't made a mistake," Lazz announced from the doorway. He stepped inside his office and crossed to where his grandmother sat. Leaning down, he gave her a kiss on each of her cheeks. "Did you bring the ring?"

She nodded unhappily. "Lazzaro…are you sure? Marco claims—"

"You took Caitlyn Vaughn from me," Marco interrupted, fury ripping through him in the face of Lazz's absolute calm. "You had to know something had happened between us or you'd never have gone to such lengths."

Lazz gave a careless shrug. "You're right. Based on how Caitlyn greeted me, I knew immediately that you'd been up to your usual tricks. Fortunately for me, she has no idea we're twins or that I wasn't the one in the lobby that morning."

Marco took a step closer to his brother and balled his

hands into fists. "Maybe I should rearrange your face a bit so she has an easier time telling us apart from now on."

Bull's-eye. More than a hint of irritation slid out from behind Lazz's impervious facade. "Last time we fought over a woman, I ended up with a scar. One from you is plenty, thanks."

"Has she seen it?" He'd have given anything to call back the words the instant they'd been uttered, especially when Lazz offered a lazy smile of confirmation in response. "You son of a—"

"Marco!" Nonna interrupted sharply.

Lazz's voice cut across the reprimand, aimed straight at his brother. "Let me explain something to you. You have this insane notion that I've somehow taken Caitlyn from you. For your information she's not mine to take, any more than she's yours. She's her own person and will make her own decision about who she will or won't date." He paused deliberately. "Or who she will or won't marry."

Marco fought to maintain control. Where he preferred action, Lazz chose reason. Long, hard experience had taught Marco that when it came to a war of logic, his only chance at winning was to keep his temper in check. And when that failed, beat his brother to a bloody pulp. Right now, that struck him as the most satisfying option. If he could find a way to maneuver Nonna out of the room, he might just give it a shot. Until then, words were all he had available.

"You told the family you'd experienced The Inferno with her," Marco accused. "You and I both know that's a lie."

"As is The Inferno."

"Lazzaro!" Nonna lifted a trembling hand to her throat. "How can you say such a thing?"

He stooped beside her chair. "I'm sorry to hurt you, Nonna, but I don't believe in The Inferno. I think it's a very sweet, very romantic fairy tale to rationalize allowing a passionate nature to overcome common sense. Sev used it to justify blackmailing a top jewelry designer into leaving our main competitor. Marco wants to use it in order to coax a Dantes employee into his bed. And Primo used it as an excuse to steal his best friend's fiancée. The Inferno doesn't exis—"

To Marco's shock, Nonna did something he'd never seen her do before. She slapped Lazzaro, stopping his words. Tears flooded her eyes. "Not another word," she ordered in Italian, before drawing a shaky breath. "Marco is right. This woman is not your soul mate. If you had felt The Inferno for her, you could not say the things you have here today. You mock and dismiss what you have never experienced. How dare you assume you know more about what happened between your grandparents and brothers than those of us involved. How dare you accuse us of lying."

Lazz's jaw tightened. "Not lying. Merely attempting to rationalize irrational emotion."

"Is what you feel for Caitlyn rational?" Marco demanded.

Lazz slowly rose to face his brother. Nonna's slap had left its mark. A light streak of red kissed the curve of his jaw. "Of course it is. Emotional attraction is quite rational. And I'm attracted to Caitlyn physically and intellectually, as well as emotionally. But I'm not going to try and pretend that what I feel for her is due to some family curse."

"Blessing," Marco and Nonna corrected in unison.

He dismissed that with a wave of his hand. "What I'm feeling are the normal sensations men and women have experienced toward one another since Adam and Eve first bumped into each other in the Garden of Eden."

"You're in love with Caitlyn Vaughn?" Marco questioned tightly.

"Are you?" Lazz shot back. "You met her once. Spoke to her for all of five minutes. And now you're trying to tell me that she's...what? Your Inferno bride?"

Anger flared anew. "Not trying. I am telling you. You've deliberately kept us apart. You had no business doing that."

Lazz waved that aside. "Oh, please. You go through women faster than Nonna's pan forte. All I did was save her from heartache."

"While taking her for yourself."

To Marco's fury, his brother simply smiled. "Now that Nonna's brought me the ring I requested, I plan to propose to her tonight. It's up to her whether or not she accepts. Considering how alike she and I are, I think we'll suit very well. Oh, she probably won't accept right away. It's much too soon and much too fast. But if nothing else, it will cement our relationship until she does agree to my proposal."

"Please, Lazzaro," Nonna interrupted. "If you persist in following this path, you will regret it for the rest of your life."

"And I'll make sure of it," Marco added.

Lazz lifted an eyebrow. "What do you plan to do? Tell Caitlyn I have a twin? I'm sure she'll find that very interesting, but hardly life altering. Tell her it was you in the lobby on her first day of work? She and I have been dating for six weeks. Do you really think she'll care after all this time?" He shook his head. "It's too little, too late. She's committed to me now. Go find someone else to charm."

"Caitlyn is meant for me and you know it. Why else would you have worked so hard to keep us apart?"

For the first time a hint of temper sparked to life in Lazz's eyes, belying his legendary control. "You think all women are meant for you, Marco. You always have, which explains the scar I carry. Don't you remember? It's because of that day, we created a 'no poaching' rule."

"I haven't forgotten, even if you have."

"There wasn't anything between you and Caitlyn, therefore I can't be guilty of poaching." Lazz folded his arms across his chest, his stance hard and firm. "Face facts, Marco. This is the one woman you can't have, which is probably why you want her. Well, you're too late. You're just going to have to find a way to deal with losing. Caitlyn and I suit each other and you're on official notice to back off. Besides, considering how vindictive *The Snitch* has gotten these past six weeks, chances are excellent they'll get hold of this story, if you don't stop pushing, and run with it. I don't think the Romanos would be happy reading about another Dante scandal. Do you?"

Far from backing off, Marco chose to approach, determined to take on anyone and anything that threatened the bond that had formed that morning in the lobby. It didn't matter that he'd only spoken to Caitlyn for five short minutes. It could have been five seconds. The instant they'd touched, their fates were sealed. He couldn't explain it. Before it had happened to him, he'd have called it insane, just as Lazz did. But the connection that occurred that day compelled him to find Caitlyn. To take her for his own. To make her his in every way possible.

And he would.

Marco went toe-to-toe with his brother. "You let me worry about the Romanos and *The Snitch.* As for Caitlyn… Would you care to put your faith in her affections to a small test? Why don't you give me a clear field tonight and we'll see which of us ends up going home with the lady."

If Nonna hadn't stepped between the two of them, Marco didn't doubt Lazz would have hit him. "Don't mess with her, Marco. Final warning. Back off."

"And I'm warning you, Lazz. The Inferno is real. And I won't let any man take my woman from me." He leaned in past his grandmother to give weight to his words. "Not even my own brother."

"Late, late, late!"

Caitlyn flew to the mirror for a final check, throwing a swift, desperate glance toward the clock. Five minutes. The car arrived in five minutes. Why, oh, why had Lazz chosen tonight of all nights to change the time they were to meet?

She perched her reading glasses on the end of her

nose and checked the note he'd sent a final time. He must have been in a hurry when he wrote it because she barely recognized his handwriting. It seemed bolder and less precise, more…passionate. And how amusing was that after her conversation with the girls? Now, where were they to meet? On the balcony of Le Premier for moonlight drinks. She shoved her glasses into her hair with a smile. How romantic.

Pausing in front of the mirror, she examined her reflection a final time. She'd dressed with extra care for the Dantes' anniversary party, choosing a floor-length gown in softest lilac and applying a touch more makeup than usual. She stared at the mirror, slightly stunned at how different she looked when she wore something other than her more mundane business attire. The makeup added a hint of glamour and sophistication, while the halter top drew attention to her shoulders and bustline. Even the sweeping skirt gave an illusion of magic and romance, floating around her like wisps of fog. Then she grinned. Her reading glasses, however, were another story.

She carefully removed them from where she'd tucked them into her upswept hair and tossed them onto her bed beside her purse. She'd have to remember to grab them before she left or she'd be depending on Lazz to read anything put in front of her tonight.

Thinking of Lazz caused her smile to falter a shade. She knew Britt and Angie believed he planned to propose sometime this evening, but they couldn't be more wrong. Her friends weren't aware that matters between her and Lazz simply hadn't progressed to that point. Her chin firmed. Until now.

Thanks to her lunchtime conversation she'd decided the time had come for a change. She wanted Lazz to make love to her, something she'd hesitated to agree to up to this point. But after some long, hard consideration, she decided she needed to know, once and for all, whether their connection went deeper than the light-hearted romance they currently shared.

She needed to know if Lazz had any Zorro in his soul.

Turning away from the mirror, she checked the clock once more and gave in to panic. She hated, hated, hated being late. Thanks to a last-minute change in Lazz's plans for the evening, she'd have to run to avoid that horror. Thank goodness for the car he told her he'd send or she wouldn't have had a hope of making it to the hotel on time. And she wanted to make it on time, to wallow in every minute of the promised romantic rendezvous before the start of his grandparents' anniversary party. Snatching up her purse, she hurried outside to the waiting car and a night that she hoped would change her entire future.

The instant she entered the hotel lobby, a uniformed employee approached. After confirming her identity, he escorted her along a corridor that ran parallel to the ballroom and gestured her through an archway that opened onto the starlit darkness of a large balcony overlooking downtown San Francisco. She paused for an instant so her eyes could adjust, then instantly realized she didn't need her eyesight. Another sense kicked in, a keen awareness of someone's presence just off to her left. An odd fever began to sizzle through her veins, flaring to life in a way that caught her by surprise. She hadn't experienced anything like this since…

She inhaled sharply. Since the morning she'd stepped through the front doors of Dantes and first met Lazz.

A smile built across her mouth. "I can feel you," she whispered into the darkness. "I can't see you, but I can feel you." She slowly turned until she faced him, or faced where she'd have bet a month's salary he stood. "Well? Aren't you going to say anything?"

"I've been waiting for you," he simply replied.

Three

Just that one comment, and yet Caitlyn's nerve endings fired to life with a fierceness that stunned her. She shivered in reaction. They were the same words Lazz had used when she'd first met him in the lobby of Dantes. How many times had they spoken since? How many times had they been together in other settings, if not quite this ripe with romance? And yet, just that one sentence succeeded in knocking her totally off-kilter.

Perhaps it had to do with his voice. It sounded deeper than all those other times. Huskier. More passionate than she'd ever heard it, and fused with blatant desire. Every feminine instinct she possessed responded to that unspoken command, urging her to go to him. To surrender. To give herself as completely and fully as only a woman can.

She took an impulsive step in his direction. *This* was the man she'd met all those weeks ago. The man who'd roused her from sleep and ignited emotions she never even realized she possessed.

"Where have you been?" she asked.

He stepped from the shadows and approached. If he found her question peculiar, he didn't let on. If anything, she suspected he understood precisely what she asked. "Does it matter? I'm here now." He held out his hand. "I have a question to ask you."

She didn't hesitate, but slipped her hand into his. *Yes!* A small voice whispered inside her head, acknowledging the rightness of his touch. Even more remarkable, she felt a surge of desire so strong and overwhelming that she couldn't think straight. Elation filled her. Here was the perfect man for her, a man who mirrored her own ideals. Practical. Safe. Successful. And powerfully alluring. All the building blocks for a successful relationship.

"What question did you want to ask?" she managed to say.

"Do you trust me?"

If he hadn't spoken with such intensity, she would have laughed. "Of course I trust you."

"Then kiss me."

She resisted the seductive lure, curiosity getting the better of her. "I don't understand. What in the world's gotten into you?"

"I'm trying to make a point. To prove that what we felt when we first touched was real. That the fantasy can become reality. That you're a woman who deserves to be swept off her feet, not just tonight, but every night."

She felt the color drain from her face. "You heard. You were in your office at lunchtime. You overheard what Britt and Angie said." Oh, God. What *she'd* said—that she was waiting for Zorro. "You heard us, didn't you?"

He inclined his head. "I did."

"I'm so sorry. I—"

"Don't apologize. It was important for me to know."

Lazz closed the distance between them and stopped her words in one easy move. Lowering his head, he cupped her face between his hands and kissed her. And with that kiss he sent her tumbling to a place she'd never been before.

He'd kissed her any number of times over the past six weeks, but it had never been anything like this. The first taste came slow and delicious, a slide of lips mingling with a whisper of tongue, combined with a bone-melting sensuality that Lazz had kept hidden from her until now. It had all the newness of a first kiss, which she found as strange and bewildering as it was utterly enchanting.

She sank into the embrace, opening to him, engaging in an escalating thrust and parry that caused a delicious friction to thrum through her veins. Why had she hesitated all these weeks? Why had she held him at arm's length? This is what she wanted. This is want she needed. If Lazz had kissed her with such sweet aggression right from the start—as she'd half anticipated after their first meeting—she would have tumbled into his bed on their first date.

He drew back ever so slightly. "Better?"

"Like night and day," she confessed. Her brows drew

together. "But I don't understand. Why didn't you kiss me like this sooner?"

"I'm kissing you like this now."

His hands swept along her jaw before tracing the length of her neck and tripping across her bared shoulders. She shivered beneath the teasing caress, and he smiled knowingly, his expression containing a suggestive, blatantly male quality. The air hitched in her lungs and then escaped in a small gasp as his hands continued their descent, exploring her curves with undisguised enjoyment. He gazed down at her as he drew her close once again, joining them together in seamless perfection.

His face eased into a slight blur thanks to her farsightedness, but she could still tell that his eyes never left hers as he held her, consuming her with their intensity. And then the color changed, burnished with brilliant sparks of amber and brown and a hint of green. In all the weeks they'd been together, she'd never seen the expression they currently displayed, a heady combination of passion, longing and determination. Nor had she ever reacted this way when he held her, as though she'd been lost and had finally found her way home.

The discrepancy bewildered her. She didn't understand it, any more than she understood what had gotten into Lazz. But whatever had transformed him, she hoped it never went away. If she had any doubts about their relationship before tonight, they dissipated beneath that one single kiss.

"All of this is because you overheard my conversation at lunch?" she asked, dazed.

He didn't deny it. "You want Zorro? I can give him to you. You want to be swept away? I can do that, too."

"Oh, Lazz." For some reason he flinched, possibly from the compassion in her voice. "I don't want you to change who you are. I just want you to be yourself." In truth, his extravagant promises shook her. Men who sold fairy tales went the way of Cinderella's carriage at midnight. Poof. She had no desire to be stuck holding a pumpkin like her grandmother.

"Believe it or not, I am being myself."

Her mouth curved into a slight smile. "You're Zorro at heart?"

"More than you can possibly imagine."

She didn't bother arguing with him. She'd spent enough time with Lazz to know that he wasn't Zorro. Zorro's brother, perhaps, but he struck her as too dispassionate and analytical to embody the mysterious swashbuckler, no matter how much she might wish it otherwise.

"I can live without Zorro," she reassured him. "At least I can if I have you." She tightened her arms around his neck. "Like this."

"You can, on one condition."

"Name it."

"That you come away with me. Right now. Tonight." He stopped her automatic refusal with a single shake of his head. "Listen to me, Caitlyn. I know you, the real you. You may cling to facts and figures and charts and graphs because they seem safe and familiar and logical. But you don't want safe or familiar or—God forbid— logical in a lover. You long for a man who sees beneath the surface, who realizes that you have the soul of a romantic and fulfills all your most passionate fantasies."

She stared at him, stunned. It was as though he'd looked inside her heart and read her deepest secrets. She'd spent a lifetime doing the "right" thing. Following the rules and toeing every one of the lines her grandmother had laid down for her. Just once she wanted to step over a line. To take a risk. And now here was Lazz, a man she was wildly attracted to, offering the chance to do just that.

"Where do you want to go?" she asked, inching closer to that line.

"Forever, Nevada."

She blinked. "You want to go to Nevada. Tonight." At his silent nod, she stared at him in confusion. "But why? If you want to spend the night together—"

He stiffened. "Go on."

For some reason she reddened. "I know we haven't… Yet. But we don't have to go all the way to Nevada for that."

He relaxed enough to laugh. "There are other reasons to go there."

She lifted an eyebrow. "You want to see a show? Gamble?"

"No, *cara*. I want to marry you."

Marco could see he'd shocked her. She stared at him, her eyes huge and dark with disbelief. "Marry me!"

He spoke from the heart. "From the moment I saw you, I wanted you. I knew you were the one."

"But these past six weeks—"

He'd anticipated that question when he'd planned

the evening. "What would you have done if I'd tried to sweep you away that first day?"

"Run like hell."

"And now, after six weeks?"

"I'm not running," she conceded. "But I am stunned. This isn't something we should leap into blindly."

"You want me." He didn't phrase it as a question.

"I can't deny that." She sank against him and pressed her cheek to his shoulder. The silken strands of her hair brushed against the line of his jaw, and he inhaled the heady fragrance. "But marriage? So soon?"

"Waiting isn't going to change my feelings for you."

"But it will give us time to get to know each other better." She pulled back a few inches. "Be practical, Lazz." Then she laughed. "What am I saying? Other than myself, you're the most practical person I've ever met."

Every time she used his brother's name, he longed to correct her, to demand that she see him...*him,* not Lazz. Soon she would. But first he had to get her to Nevada. All the arrangements he'd set into motion tonight hinged on that single point. The note he'd sent asking her to meet him a full hour ahead of the time she'd originally arranged to meet Lazz, the timetable of car and plane, the excuses Nonna would offer his brother regarding Caitlyn's failure to appear at the party—they all depended on his ability to charm one simple agreement from the woman before him.

"You had practical," he argued, "and it didn't make you any happier than it made me. It's not what I want and it sure as hell isn't what you want, either."

"Okay, I admit it," she confessed with a sigh. "I'd like more than practical."

"Then, come with me."

She teetered on the brink of surrender. "What about your grandparents' anniversary party?" She shook her head. "Let's not rush this. We can go to Nevada another time. We should be here for their special night."

"I already told Nonna about my plans in case you agreed, and we have her and Primo's complete approval. She'll make our excuses to the rest of the family." And with luck, keep Lazz running in circles until far too late. "Say yes, Caitlyn," he coaxed. "You want to be swept away and that's what I'm offering to do."

Before she could marshal any further arguments, he kissed her again. There was nothing new or tentative about this one. This kiss was a taking, powerful and physical. A demand. A seduction. A union. Never again would she mistake him for another man. Even if Lazz were to walk out onto the balcony this very moment and gather her into his arms and kiss her, he'd leave her wanting. Leave her with a bone-deep dissatisfaction coupled with an awareness that she belonged to another.

"Trust me, Caitlyn. Take a chance."

She stared at him in a total daze and he barely managed to suppress a smile. She looked like he felt. If he'd had any doubt at all about his plans for the next twenty-four hours, they'd vanished the minute she'd joined him on the balcony. From the instant they'd touched, a certainty took hold. They belonged together. He'd never been more positive of anything in his life.

"I'd like to go to Forever with you." She shook her head as though clearing it, and her hair slipped from its elegant knot to swirl about her shoulders. "But not to marry you," she hastened to add, fumbling with the pins she'd used to anchor the weighty length.

"We'll see."

"I'm serious, Lazz. No marriage."

"So am I, Caitlyn." He took the pins from her and dropped them into his pocket before stealing another kiss and practically inhaling her soft moan. "I want you for my wife."

He didn't give her an opportunity to argue, but escorted her from the balcony and out of the hotel. He'd ordered the car that had brought her to Le Premier to wait for them right outside the door so they'd have it instantly available to drive them to the airport. He'd also arranged for the corporate jet to be standing by for their trip to Nevada.

He didn't want to risk any delays that might give Caitlyn an opportunity to have second thoughts. Once they were married, he'd deal with the inevitable fallout when she discovered his true identity. But right now, he'd bind her to him with the most sacred commitment of all.

The instant they were airborne, he handed her a flute of a particularly fine sparkling wine from the Franciacorta territory in Italy. The lights in the cabin were dim and the seats wide and plush. They'd lifted the armrest separating them and sat joined at the hip with Caitlyn closest to the window. Outside the aircraft, the moon and the stars peeked in at them. He leaned toward her and kissed the dampness from her lips, all the while struggling to keep his hands to himself until a more appropriate time and place.

"Comfortable?"

"Mmm. I can't remember the last time I felt this good."

"I think I can improve on that."

"Not possible."

Without a word, he slipped an arm under her knees and swiveled her so her spine rested against the wall of the cabin and her feet were cushioned in his lap. He slipped off her high heels and let them drop to the floor. Then he wrapped his hands around the arch of her foot and began to massage her feet. He watched in amusement as she tightened her grip around her champagne flute and closed her eyes on a breathless sigh.

"I think I'd like to revisit your previous offer," she said.

His laugh rumbled softly. "I assume you'd like to make a counteroffer?"

"Absolutely." She peeked at him from beneath her lashes. "If we get married, will this be part of our evening ritual?"

"Anything you want, *cara.*"

"Why didn't you explain this particular advantage before now? All these weeks of working together and you never— Oh, that reminds me."

She switched to business mode with such ease he figured it had to come from long practice. Slipping her feet from his lap, she set aside her champagne and rifled through her purse for her PDA. "And where did I stick my reading glasses?" she muttered. "Oh, damn. I left them on the bed, after all. Listen, I nearly forgot to tell you. The Reed account called about setting up a meeting for Thursday. I wondered if I could borrow Lassiter—"

She broke off when he took the PDA from her hands

and dropped it back into her purse. "Not tonight, Caitlyn. No cell phones. No PDAs. Tonight is for romance. Not another word of business. Instead, I want to hear about your version of happily-ever-after. What does it look like, feel like? I want to know the woman, not the exec. What are your dreams?"

She blinked at him in frank astonishment. "Excuse me? How many romantic evenings have we talked shop over a bottle of Chianti? I thought that was what you preferred."

Tension filled him. "Do you want to spend your life with a business partner or with a lover? When the sun sets on our day, does it set with us discussing the Reed account, or will we be exchanging the sort of intimate details about ourselves that only lovers can share?"

Her eyes grew dark with an emotion he couldn't quite put his finger on. Something between nervousness and hope. "You're serious about this, aren't you?"

"Very serious. In fact, I want to ask you a question. A serious question."

"You can ask me anything. You know that."

"Do you believe in love at first sight...at first touch?"

"At first touch?" Her expression gentled and she slipped her hand into his. "Are you aware you're massaging your palm the same way I do?"

"I...what?"

"Your palm. Ever since we first shook hands and felt that odd spark. I catch myself massaging it. I didn't think you ever did, but you've done it twice so far tonight."

"You're right." He could have told her it was a reaction to The Inferno, one he didn't realize any of the women shared. At least, none had to date. But she wouldn't understand. Not yet. "Do you ever wonder about the day we first met?"

"All the time," she confessed softly. "I thought I'd imagined it."

He tried to curb the intensity behind his question so he wouldn't alarm her. "Why?"

She shrugged uneasily. "You know."

He'd made her uncomfortable, no doubt because she didn't want to hurt his feelings. "Because I changed after that."

"I understood," she hastened to reassure. "I'm an employee in your family's business. It wouldn't have been appropriate that day to—" She broke off with another shrug.

"To take what we'd started in the lobby to its inevitable conclusion?"

To his amusement, she avoided his gaze. "Discreetly phrased, but yes. We both know where matters were headed that morning."

"What do you think would have happened if instead of walking on to that elevator and pushing the button for personnel, you'd gone with me?"

Her head shot up and this time she gave him a direct look. "Neither of us would have reported for work that day. I'd probably have been fired and you'd have…"

"Have what?" he prompted.

"You would have found my behavior totally inappropriate. We'd have had an interesting day and I'd be working elsewhere." Her smile wavered. "And we wouldn't be sitting here discussing it."

"I have another scenario." He forked his fingers deep into her hair and tilted her face up toward his. "I think we would have slipped away and allowed what we felt for each other to reach its natural conclusion. And then I would have called personnel and explained that I'd misappropriated you on official Dantes business and that you would begin work the next day."

"That's a nice fantasy."

He shook his head. "It's what should have happened. Instead I almost lost you. What happened in the lobby became nothing more than a dream, one that faded with each passing day until you began to think you'd imagined the connection we forged that morning."

"But it's back now," she reminded him with a misty smile. "So it's all good."

"And it's going to stay good. Because this time we're listening to our instincts, instead of running from them."

"And when reality intrudes?"

"I want you to promise me you'll keep listening to those instincts. That you'll follow your heart instead of your head."

She laughed again, louder and more freely than before, which pleased him no end. "I can't believe you of all people are telling me that, Lazzaro Dante."

He stiffened at the name. "And why is that?"

"Oh, please. Just yesterday you were explaining that emotion and instinct weren't to be trusted. That the reason we get along so well is because we're both rational, logical people." A frown creased her brow. "What's changed your mind since then?"

"I'm surprised you bought into that load of horse manure," he replied, attempting to turn it into a joke.

She persisted, her eyes narrowing. "You're the one who said it. Don't you believe it?"

"Not even a little."

"Well, I do…did. Now I'm really confused." A hint of tension underscored her comment. "What's going on, Lazz?"

"Caitlyn…" He needed to find a way to put them on a different footing than the one she shared with his brother. "I'd like to start over. Right here and right now. For the rest of this trip, let's pretend it's that first morning again and we've just met. Do you think you can do that?"

"I suppose." The tension seeped away little by little. "Actually, it sounds like fun."

To Marco's relief, Caitlyn took his suggestion to heart and accepted, where before she'd questioned. The attendant approached just then to inform them they were about to land. Once again he'd arranged for a car to take them to their hotel, a gorgeous rambling structure beside a small, sparkling lake. They were immediately escorted to a private suite, one with acres of bed, a sunken bathtub, a whirlpool that could have doubled as a swimming pool and a private balcony complete with hot tub.

He turned to her and grinned. "Which one do you want to get naked in first?"

Four

Caitlyn simply stood and stared at the amenities in utter disbelief. "My entire apartment could fit into that bathtub."

"Hmm. Sounds like you need a larger apartment. Maybe we can do something about that when we return. My place is at least as large as that bed. What do you say, *cara?* Interested in swapping a tub for a bed?"

She spun around to face him. "You know, that's the third time tonight you've called me by that endearment, which is really strange considering you haven't used it since the morning we first met. In fact, I've heard you use more Italian in the past couple hours than in the past couple weeks."

"Get used to it. Passion brings it out in me." He looked around with almost boyish enthusiasm and rubbed his hands together. "Let's try out everything.

Where do you want to start? A long, romantic soak with candles and chocolates? A spin in the hot tub?" His voice deepened. "Or should we play hide-and-seek on that football-field-size bed?"

"Lazz—"

He couldn't help it. His brother's name on Caitlyn's lips sent him straight over the edge. He needed to find a way of separating the two of them in her mind, to put an indelible mark on her that could never be erased. "The bed it is."

He reached her side in two easy strides and scooped her up in his arms. She shivered within his hold, trepidation warring with desire. He saw the instant desire won. It leaked into her eyes and tinted her cheeks a gentle rose. It trembled on her lips and rippled endlessly through her, turning her soft and pliant. With the quietest of sighs, she wrapped her arms around his neck and buried her face in the crook of his shoulder.

"I don't want to be a high-powered business exec anymore," she informed him in a muffled voice.

He felt unbearably tender toward the woman in his arms. "Who would you like to be?"

"Me. Right now. With you." She lifted her head to look at him with an endearingly solemn expression. "What could be more perfect?"

"Nothing that I can think of."

He stripped back the plush comforter and blanket before easing her onto the mattress. Her hair spilled like black ink across sheets of baby-soft ivory cotton, the ebony strands as soft as spun silk. He came down beside her, in no hurry now that he had her where he most wanted her.

"We could make this trip even more special, if you want," he offered gently. "When we return tomorrow, it could be as Mr. and Mrs. Dante."

For a split instant he thought he'd pushed an inch too far. Staring up at him, she moistened her lips. "You know," she admitted hesitantly. "I'd planned how I'd answer you tonight, just in case Britt and Angie were right about your intentions."

"And what did you decide?"

"To tell you how much I appreciated our friendship and hoped over time it could become more than that. More intimate than that." The explanation sounded more like a confession. "That I was willing to take the next step if you were, but that we'd have to take it slowly."

"And now?"

Tears sparkled like diamonds in her eyes. "And now all I can think about is how lucky I am to have found you again and how afraid I am that I'll wake up tomorrow and it'll just be a lovely dream. That our relationship will go back to the way it was and I'll lose all this."

"This isn't a dream and you're not going to lose me."

The apprehension lingered, a shadow that darkened the clear blue of her eyes. "What happens if everything changes again? What happens if we revert to how we were before?"

"That won't happen, I promise." He feathered a kiss across her mouth. "Marry me, Caitlyn, and I'll fill your days and nights with more romance and adventure than your wildest dreams."

"Considering some of my dreams, that's a pretty tall order."

"Try me."

Joy welled upward and she nodded. "I do believe you just won yourself a bride, Mr. Dante."

"Are you sure?"

"Very sure."

"Then, what do you say we do this right?" He checked his watch. "The marriage bureau doesn't close until midnight—"

Her arms tightened around his neck. "And how do you know that?"

"*Cara,*" he admonished, laying on a thick Italian accent. "It's my great pleasure to anticipate your every need."

"Which you're doing brilliantly."

"Which I'll soon do even more brilliantly. Let me make a quick phone call and then we'll go for our license."

"Perfect. That'll give me time to freshen up."

She didn't shift from her position, but simply gazed at him with such yearning that Marco knew that if he didn't get them off the bed and fast, they wouldn't leave it anytime soon. He risked another kiss, sliding across the lushness of her mouth before dipping inward. Just a gentle give and take, a lazy teasing duel that teetered on the edge of flaming out of control.

She broke off the kiss with a strangled moan. "I don't understand any of this. It's like kissing an entirely different person."

That had him levering off the bed. He softened his desertion by holding out his hand with a warm smile.

"Come on. Now that you've said yes, I want to turn my brand-new bride-to-be into my brand-new wife."

She sat up, delightfully appealing in her rumpled state. He'd done that to her. He'd upended her neat little columns and smudged all her meticulous facts and figures. And she'd let him. More, she'd encouraged him to yank her outside her box and into his world, a world without order or logic. It did, however, have a plan, one he'd executed with all the care and precision of his twin brother.

"A bride-to-be and a wife, all in one night." She wrinkled her nose. "I'm not sure it gets much crazier than that."

"Give it time," he said, hoping she missed the irony underscoring his comment.

While Caitlyn freshened up, Marco placed a phone call to confirm the arrangements for their wedding, arrangements that would, he hoped, make the night as special as possible. The trip to and from the marriage bureau took hardly any time at all, though filling out the necessary forms gave Marco a moment's worry. Fortunately, since Caitlyn had forgotten her reading glasses in her rush to meet him, the forms were a total blur.

Draping an arm across her shoulder, he helped her without making it too obvious. And all the while he wondered how they'd get through the wedding ceremony. He had a serious suspicion that when she was asked if she took Marco Dante for her husband, she might take serious exception to marrying the wrong name, even if he were the right man.

Returning to the hotel, Marco found his requests had not just been met but exceeded. The small chapel overflowed with flowers of every shape, color and variety, while pure white candles gave the room a soft glow. A string quartet played in the background, filling the room with soft, romantic music. He'd asked for a priest to officiate, preferably in the Latin he'd grown up with, and discovered that even that had been arranged. And the "attendants" he'd hired to help with any special touches Caitlyn wished to make to her gown, hair or makeup were waiting to usher her to a small anteroom, while he paced nervously in front of the altar.

The minute the priest arrived, he explained the changes he wished to make to the ceremony. Come tomorrow there'd be hell to pay for this night. He'd have to deal with his wife's shock and anger when she discovered his duplicity. With his brother's fury. With his family's disapproval at the method he'd chosen to circumvent Lazz. None of that mattered. All he cared about was Caitlyn's instinctive reaction whenever he took her in his arms. Her head might not know him but every other part of her did, and responded with loving abandon. The rest would come in time.

Assuming he could convince her to give him that time.

She appeared in the doorway of the chapel just then, and he could have sworn his heart froze in his chest. He'd never seen anyone more beautiful in his life. With a shy smile she came to him, floating down the short aisle, her gown drifting around her as though spun from cobwebs. A wispy lace veil framed the elegant contours of her face, and she clutched a bouquet of simple white roses.

The ceremony proceeded as though part of a dream.

The one time the priest used Marco's name, he leaned forward an instant beforehand and whispered a teasing comment in her ear so that the discrepancy went unnoticed. Toward the end of the ceremony, he put his ring on her finger, pleased at the sharp little gasp she uttered when she saw it.

He'd chosen an exquisite fire diamond solitaire in an antique platinum setting from a selection of rings Nonna had obtained, along with matching wedding bands. "You planned this from the start didn't you?" she asked in a shaken undertone.

"Let's just say I'd hoped that when I asked, you'd agree."

Color blossomed in her cheeks. "Thank you. I don't think I've ever been happier."

He shot her a smoldering look. "Give it time. I intend to make you a lot happier in a little while."

Her color deepened, but she didn't look away. If anything her eyes held a promise he hoped would last the rest of their lives. On the dot of midnight they were pronounced husband and wife, and Marco swept Caitlyn into his arms and kissed his wife for the first time.

Afterward they returned to their suite. "Would you like another glass of wine?" he asked, stripping off his suit jacket.

She gently set her bouquet on a side table and ran her fingertip across the velvety blossoms. "I don't want the wine blurring my memory." She lifted her gaze to his. "You do want me to remember everything, don't you?"

He could feel his body clench in anticipation. "Every minute," he confirmed.

Heat fired in her eyes. "Then I'll pass on the champagne."

For his own peace of mind, he had to be certain. "Does it bother you that we've rushed things? That we didn't have our family here?"

She shook her head. "Not really. Gran is gone now, and I haven't a clue where my mother is these days."

"Why not?" he asked without thinking.

She stilled, staring at him strangely. "You know why, Lazz."

"Right. Sorry." He snagged his jacket from where he'd discarded it, and crossed to the far side of the suite to hang it up, using that as an excuse to conceal his expression. "I'm afraid there's going to be hell to pay from my side of the family," he offered from the depths of the closet.

To his relief the dangerous moment passed and she focused on this latest concern. "They'll be upset they weren't invited, won't they?"

"We're not the first in the family to elope. But they won't be pleased, no."

"Especially since it wasn't necessary."

He took instant exception. "On the contrary. I think it was very necessary. I think we needed to get away from work and family and just trust what we feel for each other." He cocked his head to one side. "Don't you?"

She gave it a moment's serious consideration before nodding. "I'm beginning to suspect it wouldn't have worked out between us otherwise." A swift smile came and went. "Too much brick and not enough mortar."

"The mortar being the romance?"

She nodded and satisfaction filled Marco. His brother had been so wrong about her, as were Britt and Angie. Caitlyn and Lazz were nothing alike. Granted, they both shared an accountant mentality. But that was about as far as it went. Inside, where it counted, she epitomized all that was most female. The monumental spirit, the softness covering indomitable strength, the brilliance tempered by compassion and creativity. They were qualities that had gotten lost at Dantes. Qualities his brother had neither noticed nor understood.

But Marco understood them. Savored them. Intended to revel in them from this moment forward. He took his time, determined to make this night the most special possible. He slowly approached, ripping free his tie and unbuttoning his shirt as he came.

"Tell me what you're feeling, Caitlyn."

"Happy. Nervous." Her gaze dropped to his bared chest. "Hungry."

He continued to close the distance between them. "The first I intend to feed. The second I can appease. And the third I plan to fully satisfy. On every level."

He reached her side and cradled her against him, kissing away any lingering doubts until she shuddered helplessly, the want in her so huge, it couldn't be contained. "Wait," he murmured. "First things first." He removed the veil, using more than his usual care, and draped it across the back of a nearby chair.

Caitlyn stood silently, waiting for him. And then she wasn't waiting. She slid into his embrace and slanted her mouth over his in a hot, greedy kiss, one that told him in no uncertain terms how much she wanted him. He found the fastening for her gown at the nape of her neck and flicked it open. The edges of the halter top fluttered to her waist, baring her to his gaze. Without a word, she reached behind her and unzipped the gown, allowing it to drift to the floor before she stepped clear of it.

She wore nothing but a minuscule triangle of lace that barely concealed the heart of her femininity. She should have appeared provocative. Instead she struck him as proud and elegant, and more desirable than any woman he'd ever known. He took his time, looking his fill until he realized that beneath her calm facade, his lovely wife felt nervous. Maybe he'd have caught on sooner if he'd known her a little longer, if they'd shared some of those bricks she'd referred to. The reminder had a frown cutting across his face.

"I can fix that for you," he offered.

Bewilderment momentarily eclipsed her apprehension. "Fix what?"

He captured her hand in his and opened her bunched fingers one by one. "This."

She shut her eyes in chagrin and blew out a sigh. "Gave myself away, didn't I?"

"Just a bit." He drew her against him, allowing the heat from his body to sooth the tautness from hers. Slow and easy, he reminded himself. "Tell me what you're worried about."

"It's a long list," she confessed.

He shrugged. "We have all night." He sent his fingers on a dance of exploration, one along the smooth length of her spine, the other across the fragile bones of her shoulder blades. "First problem?"

She shuddered beneath his touch, and to his amusement it took her a moment to gather her thoughts. If he didn't miss his guess, that was a novel experience for his new bride. "I...it's just the speed of all this, I suppose," she explained with a shrug. "Just a couple hours ago we were in San Francisco on the balcony—"

"And I promised you a moonlit drink that we never quite got around to." He skated his mouth along the path his hand had taken, kissing his way from the curve of her shoulder to the base of her throat. There he paused. "Well, that's not quite true. We did have a drink on the plane. And there was a moon peering in on us. Did you notice it?"

"The moonlight was perfect and I had my drink," she managed to reply. As though unable to help herself, her head dipped to one side to offer him better access. "But how did we end up here? We were just supposed to share a romantic interlude before the anniversary party."

"Which is what we're doing right now. Unless you want to stop interluding?" He nuzzled her ear, catching the lobe between his teeth. Slowly he tugged. "Yes? No?"

The breath hissed from her lungs in reaction. "No, don't stop. Just explain to me how we went from there to here."

"Ah. You want logic." He smiled against her heated skin at her attempt to bring order to disorder. Since when was romance and passion logical? "Let me guess.... You want a map of points and coordinates so you can trace your path from point A to point Z."

His teasing eased something within her. He sensed the slight loosening as humor defeated tension. "Something like that."

He slanted his mouth over hers until nothing existed for either of them but the play of their lips and tongue. "I can do that for you." He lifted her hand and brushed a kiss in its center. "For your information, this is point A, the place we first touched."

She gasped for air. "Oh, right. I remember now. *That's* where this all started."

He didn't give her time to recover her breath. He swung her into his arms and carried her to the bed. "And right here is point Z." He followed her down onto the mattress. "There are a few other miscellaneous points in between." He dismissed them with a wave of his hand. "But you get the general idea."

"Lazz—"

He nearly swore out loud at her use of his brother's name, knowing full well he had no one to blame for that but himself. Aware of her watchful gaze, he managed a teasing smile. "Would you like to go back to point A, or is Z good enough for you."

She pretended to consider. "Z, please. With a few Gs, Rs and Ws thrown in for good measure."

"Excellent suggestion, *cara*. I'm particularly good at W."

"I know I had a long list of other worries, but right now I can't think of a single one." Her hand feathered across the planes of his face. "All I want is for you to prove how well you do W."

"My pleasure."

She lay beneath him, a veritable palette of subtle colors. The flush of palest rose against a sweeping canvas of ivory curves. Lips a shade just shy of coral.

The tips of her breasts a shade deeper than her lips. Against all that flowed the black of darkest night, the rippling waves of her hair striking a sharp contrast to the expanse of pastel. And finally there was the brilliant teal blue of her eyes, staring at him as though the sun rose and set at his command.

Would she still feel that way about him tomorrow? If not, that only gave him tonight, a night he intended to make as perfect as possible. He gathered her hands in his and guided them to his chest, and where she explored his body, so he explored hers, mirroring each and every move.

A smile of delight appeared the instant she caught on to his game. She deliberately ran her fingers along the sculpted muscles of his chest, circling the flat discs of his nipples. Her eyes widened when he did the same to her, eliciting a choked gasp.

"Is this how you want to play?" she demanded when she'd recovered sufficiently to speak.

"We'll see who caves first."

She lifted an eyebrow. "So the loser is the one who cries uncle first?"

"Trust me. There are no losers in this game." He flashed her a swift grin. "Unless you count losing out on bragging rights."

But he could tell he'd intrigued her and he could see the determination build in her, the desire to have him be the first to put an end to this novel form of foreplay. "We'll see who's bragging come morning," she muttered.

He didn't want to think about tomorrow. Only tonight mattered. He lowered his head to her breast and captured her nipple between his teeth, tugging gently. Her soft cry was all he could have asked for and more. When she didn't immediately reciprocate, he asked, "Giving up, already?"

Then it was his turn to shudder, his turn to struggle to master his self-control. She played the game better than he'd anticipated, proving more creative than logical, which only confirmed his suspicions about her. Even so, he didn't think what was happening between them had to do with creativity, alone. He'd never been touched with such attentiveness or such open curiosity before. And he suddenly realized that she was having fun, almost as though such playfulness were a rare treat for her. Almost as though her life had been all work, with far too little play.

"You're laughing," he accused at one point.

She struggled to control herself, failing miserably. "Do you mind? I swear it's not at you. I've just never tried this game before."

"And you're enjoying it."

"I really am."

The bed became their playground. At some point, his trousers and boxers vanished. He used the opportunity to switch off all but one of the lights, a lamp that bathed the room in soft shadows. He returned to the bed and rolled with her to the darkest section of the bed, where the light couldn't betray that he lacked the scar his brother carried. And then the game turned serious.

He started the chase again, intent on pushing her over the edge. As though picking up on the change, her laughter faded, replaced by an escalating passion.

Where before his hands tripped across her skin, now they sought out the areas he'd discovered to be the most sensitive. The back of her knees. The inside of her thigh just below the panty line. The silken slope of her belly. The dimpled hollow above her backside. And along her side where taut skin became soft breast. He gave each and every section of her body his full attention. Gave to her, pleasure after pleasure.

"You win." The breath sobbed from her lungs. "Please, make love to me. I can't wait any longer. Make love to me now."

"I only win if you win."

She fisted her hands in his hair and drew him down to her, in a long open-mouthed kiss. He'd removed her panties at some point during their game and she opened herself for his possession, encouraging him without words to give completion to the escalating passion that had been building between them.

He threaded his fingers with hers, locking them together palm to palm. This is where The Inferno had first burned, and he could feel it there still, uniting them just as he planned to unite their bodies. He whispered her name as he slid inward. Taking, giving, melding.

Gently, he possessed her. Then not so gently. She reared up to meet him, incandescent in her passion. The urgency grew, bit hard. She called to him, urging him on. Pleading. Demanding. Laughing and crying. He'd never experienced with another woman anything close to what he did in that moment with Caitlyn. Not like this. Never like this.

He could feel the building. Feel the ending approach.

He wanted to snatch it back. To live in this moment forever, until the pleasure ripped them both apart. And then it did. She fisted around him, her climax careening through her, surging in wild, crashing waves. Unable to help himself, he crashed with her.

Together they tumbled into an aftermath of weak, tangled limbs and quiet bits of lovespeak that made no sense but somehow maintained the emotional connection. Marco wound his arms around his bride, his wife, this soul mate The Inferno had given him, and rolled them into a warm ball that wedded soft with hard in a timeless blending of opposites.

He couldn't remember how long they slept. He woke once more during the night and they made love again, this time long and languid. The game they'd played gave them a greater awareness of each other's wants and needs and added a depth and power to their lovemaking.

The second time he woke, he felt the advent of morning. Slipping from the bed, he crossed first to the coffeemaker and turned it on and then to the bathroom where he opened the faucet full force. He picked up a jar of bath salts and removed the lid, sniffed, then upended a goodly portion into the water. Foam erupted. Satisfied, he padded to the sitting area to pour the coffee and transport the two steaming mugs to the tiled platform around the tub. Then he went in search of his wife, finding her, much to his pleasure, right where he'd left her.

Not a morning person, he realized the instant he lifted her from her warm cocoon. "I'm shocked you even know that word, let alone would use it to describe your husband," he said with a husky laugh.

"I know a lot more swear words and I'm going to use them if you don't take me straight back to bed."

"I have something better in mind." He maneuvered down the three short steps into the sunken tub and eased her into the water. Her shriek of surprise turned to a groan of pleasure. He chuckled. "Ah, there's the woman I married. You had me worried for a moment there."

"This feels amazing." She leaned against the sloping edge opposite him and rubbed her foot along the length of his leg. "What do you say we start every morning this way."

"I'll see what I can arrange." He handed her one of the mugs. "I wonder if we can order breakfast in here. They've been so accommodating about everything else."

"There's a phone on the wall by the tub," she said, burying her nose in the mug. "See if you can reach it."

"I'm game, if you are." He levered himself upward, his fingers just glancing off the receiver. He half rose and tried again. Behind him, he heard her coffee mug clatter into the bathtub.

"Oh. God."

At first he thought she'd scalded herself and whipped around to help. And then he knew.

Time was up.

Five

"Who the hell are you?" Caitlyn demanded.

"Your husband."

"Don't treat me like a fool. You're not Lazz." She forced down the surge of hysteria battering to escape. But she couldn't keep herself from folding in on herself in an attempt to hide her nudity beneath the scant covering of rapidly dissipating bubbles. Though why she bothered after what the two of them had done last night, she couldn't say. "Lazz has a scar on his hip. I saw it when we went swimming. You don't have a scar."

"No, I don't. And no, I'm not Lazz." He slowly rose, water sheeting off him as he stepped from the tub and snagged a towel. "That doesn't change the fact that I'm your husband."

It took every ounce of self-control to keep from

totally losing it. She felt hideously exposed, and more than a little frightened. She'd married this man—a complete stranger—and didn't even know his name. She'd made love to him all through the night. Frolicked like a child in a bubble-filled bathtub. But she didn't have a clue who he was, other than a dead ringer for Lazz.

She fought to apply reason to insanity, to use what little logic and common sense remained at her disposal, while all around her bricks and mortar crumbled. "Since you look exactly like Lazz, I'm assuming you're related. His brother?" Her brain gave a kick-start. "His twin brother?"

"Yes."

"Lazz never mentioned a twin," she stated tightly. "Is this your idea of a joke? Is he in on whatever amusing little scam you're trying to pull, or is this all your own idea?"

"This isn't a joke or a scam. And if you'll look closely, you'll see I'm not the least amused. Here." He ripped another towel off the glass-and-wrought-iron rack and held it out to her. "I suspect you'll be more comfortable having this conversation if you aren't naked."

She struggled to hold tears at bay. "I can't believe I'm having his conversation at all. I want to know who the hell you are and what sort of hideous game you're playing."

Clutching the towel to her breasts, she stood and wrapped the thick length of cotton around herself. Lazz—*no, not Lazz*—cupped her elbow to steady her as she climbed out of the water. She almost thanked him before catching it back at the last instant.

"*Cara*—"

She yanked free of his hold. "Don't. Don't you dare call me that. Now, who are you?"

"Marco Dante."

"Marco." She recognized the name. Hadn't she heard Britt rhapsodize endlessly over the past six weeks about the "charming" one of the Dante brothers? Why, in the name of everything holy, had her friend neglected to mention that Marco and Lazz were twins? "How did this happen? *Why* did it happen? Does Lazz know what you've pulled?"

He removed a terry cloth robe from the back of the door without answering and handed it over. She didn't want to appreciate his thoughtfulness. She didn't want him doing or saying anything that would make her feel kindly disposed toward him. She shrugged on the robe and belted it tightly around her waist before allowing the towel to drop to the floor at her feet.

Lazz—*Marco*—didn't bother with a robe but exited into the bedroom with the towel slung carelessly around his waist. She desperately wanted him to cover up, to hide that impressive chest that she'd peppered with kisses. To conceal those amazing arms that had held her with such tender strength. To turn from mind-blowing lover back into a normal, average man, despite the fact that there wasn't and never would be anything normal or average about him.

To her relief, once they'd reached the sitting room, Marco gave her some much-needed breathing space. "First, this is no game," he began. "And it happened because Lazz gave me no other choice. At least none, given the limited amount of time I had to work with."

She held up a hand to silence him, wishing she'd chugged that coffee instead of losing it in the bathwater. Spying the coffeemaker and—hallelujah—a half pot of coffee remaining, she crossed the room and poured herself a cup. Then a second. Satisfied that her brain was firing on at least half its cylinders, she faced the man she'd married only hours earlier.

"I need you to explain things, but I need them explained in a way I can understand. So, I'm going to ask the questions and you're going to answer them, simply and concisely. Got it?"

"Logic, Caitlyn?"

She resented the knowing look in his eyes, a look accompanied by a familiar flash of humor. She lifted her chin to a combative angle. "It's what I do best. Or did, until recently," she corrected.

She struggled to come up with a logical first question, but for some reason it hovered just beyond her reach. All she could think of was that she'd been tricked into a bogus marriage by this man so that he could... Could what? Get her into bed? That didn't make a bit of sense. He didn't have to go through this sham of a wedding in order to accomplish that. Hit out at Lazz? Possibly. But...why?

She rubbed at the tension headache forming behind her temples, wishing with all her heart that she wore a business suit, had her reading glasses to hide behind and a pad of paper and pen to help organize her thoughts. "Okay, first question. Is there a rational beginning to all this? Someplace we can start from?"

"You'd like a point A?"

The poignancy of the question ripped into her, making it almost impossible to keep her voice steady enough to answer. "Yes. Point A would be an excellent place to start."

"That's easy enough." His hazel eyes grew watchful and intent, while the color darkened to autumnal flashes of gold and brown. "You and I met the morning you started at Dantes," he surprised her by saying. "In the lobby near the receptionist's desk."

She blinked in surprise. "That was you?"

"Yes." He kept his voice even, though she sensed it cost him. "I didn't realize it at the time, but apparently you thought I was Lazz."

"The receptionist," Caitlyn explained. "He told me you were Lazz. And since the head of personnel had already pointed out your brother to me during my interview. I assumed…"

"A natural mistake."

She inclined her head. "There's no reason why I'd think there might be two of you, especially since no one's mentioned anything about a twin in the interim. Maybe they thought I already knew."

"If I'd realized that, I'd have corrected the misunderstanding right then and there and it would have saved us—" he swept a negligent hand through the air "—all this."

He couldn't be more wrong. She'd heard stories about Marco, stories that ensured she'd have given short shrift to any advances coming from the sort of man cut from her grandfather's cloth. "Just to be clear? I would never get involved with a man like you."

"But we are involved, *cara*. More than involved," he

replied gently. He didn't give her time to argue his statement. "I think I know the next part of the story. Lazz
didn't bother straightening out the mix-up in the lobby.
And I was sent off on a sudden emergency. A very convenient sudden emergency."

She caught the ripple of tension whenever he mentioned his brother's name. Something had happened
there, and somehow she'd been put in the middle of it.
Before this ended she'd find a way to change that. "You
believe Lazz is responsible for your change in job assignment? Why?" She read the answer in his gaze and
shook her head in disbelief. "Because of me? You must
be joking."

Marco leaned against the archway between the
bedroom and sitting area and folded his arms across his
chest. "He wanted you," he said with a shrug. "He didn't
realize you were already taken."

"Taken!" Her temper flashed like wildfire. "Let me
clarify something for you, Mr. Dante. Despite current
evidence to the contrary, I'm not some brainless object
to be picked up or discarded or, even worse, fought over
by a pair of schoolboys. I make my own choices. I
always have and I always will."

"I'm relieved to hear that, since it means you won't give
in to whatever demands Lazz makes when he hears about
our marriage. I won't have him coming between us again."

She sucked in a breath and felt her face go white with
shock. "Dear God. Are you saying that the events of the
past twenty-four hours are your way of retaliating against
your brother?" Her voice rose despite her best attempts
to control it. "Are you kidding me? Just because he suc-

ceeded in dating someone you'd chosen for yourself? You did this to me so you could hit out at Lazz?"

He straightened, a wash of color sweeping along his elegant cheekbones. "You chose Lazz because you didn't realize we were the ones who connected that morning in the lobby. Who bonded."

"We shook hands, Marco! That was it."

"And experienced The Inferno."

She stared at him, nonplussed. "I know I'm going to regret asking this, but what's The Inferno?" He took his time, explaining in detail, and she actually found herself listening. So it had a name, came her first thought, before she downed the last of her coffee, praying it would help her make sense of what had to be total nonsense. "And you actually believe in this superstition or fantasy or whatever?"

He took instant exception. "It's not superstition or fantasy. All the Dantes believe in it. Well, except for Lazz." He considered for an instant. "And possibly Nicolò. The jury's still out on my cousins, only because they haven't had it happen to them, yet. But that's not the point, damn it. It's real. It happened to us. And before long you'll believe, as well."

She glared at him. She didn't want to accept a single word he said, even though it helped explain how she'd ended up here, married to a complete stranger. For some bizarre reason—other than The Inferno—she'd decided to chase after Zorro and gotten herself in this mess, all in the name of a little excitement. This was why steady and predictable won the race every time. Still...

She shook her head, more for her own benefit than

his. "I don't believe you. Not that it matters, because after today I'm never going to see you again."

He simply smiled. "And why would you want to do that? We're married. Did last night mean so little to you?"

To her embarrassment, the tears she'd managed to hold at bay earlier escaped. "It meant everything to me. Or it would have if you hadn't lied to me. You committed fraud. You knew full well that if you'd introduced yourself as Marco, I'd have had nothing to do with you. So you pretended to be Lazz in order to trick me into marriage. To trick me into bed. I guarantee a good lawyer will put a fast end to our marriage."

To her dismay, he approached, rousing emotions she had no business experiencing. "Yesterday your friends warned you that Lazz planned to propose at Primo and Nonna's anniversary party. Tell me, Caitlyn. What answer would you have given him if he had?"

"I don't see what that has to do—"

"You would have refused him, wouldn't you? At the very least you would have asked for time. You told me as much last night."

"Okay, fine," she conceded. "That's what I would have done. So?"

"Why did you change your mind? Why did you agree to marry me?"

"Temporary insanity combined with too much champagne."

"Ah, *cara*," he murmured with a laugh. "You can't lie to me. Last night had nothing to do with too much wine and you know it. You left the party with me, married me, made love to me, because you recognized on a visceral level that I'm the man with whom you belong. And you planned to refuse Lazz for the same reason. Just as you sensed the connection between us, you felt the lack with him."

"Why didn't you simply explain about the mix-up?" It was a cry from the heart. "Why resort to subterfuge?"

"I ran out of time," he said simply. "Lazz planned to propose and even if you'd refused him, you would have refused any advances on my part, as well. Don't you understand? He doesn't love you, sweetheart."

"And you do?"

"I'm not going to answer that because you won't believe anything I say at this point. Only time will convince you whether or not we're meant to be together. Lazz has decided that you two have enough in common to make marriage a logical choice, but that's not reasonable grounds for marriage."

"It's more reasonable than the way you went about it," she retorted. "Until last night, we'd been in each other's company for a whole five minutes. And now you've locked us into this bogus marriage."

"It's not bogus," he corrected calmly. "My legal name is on the marriage license. The priest used it during the ceremony."

She stared in dismay. "He did?"

He hesitated. "I might have distracted you about then. It's possible you weren't paying strict attention."

"Oh, Marco." Satisfaction flared to life in his eyes, brought on, she suspected, by her use of his real name. "This isn't going to work. You realize that, don't you?"

"You're right."

She opened her mouth to argue, then closed it again when his comment sank in. "I am?"

"It's not going to work if you're unwilling to take a chance."

He wrapped his arms around her. She shuddered at the familiar feel of his arms, at the scent of the oils from their bath that still clung to his bare chest. More than anything she wanted to close her eyes and return to those magical hours they'd shared the previous night. To tumble into bed with this man and sleep, secure in the certainty that all was right with her world.

Only it wasn't. Not any longer.

"I can't stay married to you. I don't *know* you."

"Yes, you do." He settled a hand over her heart. "In here you know me better than anyone. Or do you think that's not enough? That what we shared last night won't last?"

"It can't. We're strangers, Marco."

"We're lovers, Caitlyn. And in time we'll be friends and companions as well as lovers. In time we'll learn each other's secrets. We'll fight on occasion and adjust to accommodate each other. We'll talk and laugh. And all the while this bond we share, this Inferno, will bind us together until we think and feel as one. All you have to do is give our marriage a chance."

"You're asking me to build a life with you based on fairy tales and wishful thinking. There's no foundation here," she said desperately. "Sex isn't enough."

"We'll create that foundation together over time."

"What about Lazz?"

A change swept over him. Where before he'd been the ultimate charmer, now a toughness tautened muscle and sinew and struck like flint in his voice. "I'll deal with Lazz."

"He didn't do anything wrong," she urged. "He was attracted to me, just as you were."

"Don't." He moderated his tone slightly. "Don't defend him to me. What he did was carefully calculated. He knew I wanted you and deliberately intervened to keep us apart."

"I can't believe it was deliberate, Marco."

"I won't discuss this with you, Caitlyn. I just want your promise to keep your distance from now on."

"Because I'm yours now?" His silence said it all, and she fought free of his embrace. "You realize that's going to be difficult since both Lazz and I work in finance? Our paths cross on a regular basis."

"I'll take care of it."

That didn't sound good. "You'll take care of it…how?"

But he simply shook his head. "He's my brother, Caitlyn. My twin brother. He's my problem from now on."

If she were smart, she'd put an end to things right now. Walk—hell, run—in the opposite direction. But memories of their hours together intruded. Of the picture-perfect wedding and a night unlike anything she'd ever experienced before. As much as logic and reason warned her to end things, irrational desire drew Caitlyn to Marco.

As though sensing her weakness, he captured her hand in his and give a gentle tug. "Kiss me, Caitlyn. Just once. Kiss me—Marco—and not my brother."

She could read between the lines. He was asking for

what amounted to a first kiss, because in a way that's what it would be. Hurt and anger warred with a desire she couldn't suppress, no matter how she might long to. The connection he'd referred to—a connection she wanted to deny—continued to link them. Not that she believed his superstitious nonsense about The Inferno. All it did was gave a name to the uncontrollable emotions she'd experienced in the lobby. It was a pretty bow used to dress up a battered box. This was lust, not love, no matter how bright and shiny the ribbon.

Caitlyn stared at Marco, determined to turn away. But it was almost as though her body divorced itself from her brain. Without a word she wrapped her arms around his neck. She watched him closely, waiting for a glint of satisfaction or triumph. But the only emotion that came through was a stoic longing and a barely banked heat. Slowly she pulled his head down to hers and gave him the kiss he'd requested.

She'd planned to make it fast and passionless. To prove that whatever had existed between them had been destroyed by his duplicity. And she would have, except for one small problem. The instant her mouth touched his, she lost total control.

Hot, heavy desire ripped her apart while images flashed through her mind. A voice, deep with passion asking her to trust him. Soft, shared laughter. A priest blessing their union. The tenderness with which he touched her. The fun he'd somehow incorporated into the short time they spent together. The joy. The romance.

The passion.

She turned her head sharply away and shoved against

his shoulders, fighting back tears. "I can't. I can't do this."

Before he could argue, his cell phone rang. "Time to face the music," he murmured. Releasing her, he picked up his trousers and rummaged through the pockets for his phone. He flipped it open and listened for a second, then winced. "Sorry, Sev. I completely forgot I'd promised to meet with the Romanos. It'll take me a couple hours to get there. Can you postpone the meeting until after lunch?" He thrust a hand through his hair, rumpling it into appealing disarray. "Never mind where I am. You can tell Lazz— Forget it. I'll tell him myself. I'll explain everything when I get there." He ended the call and pocketed his cell. "We need to return to San Francisco."

"And then?"

Determination settled over his features. "You're my wife, Caitlyn. That hasn't changed. Since we can't go back, there's only one way to go from here." His determination solidified. "And that's forward."

It took the entire flight home for Marco to convince Caitlyn to give their marriage a chance instead of ending it precipitously. And it took the entire drive from the airport into the city to gain her promise to say nothing to Lazz until after his meeting with the Romanos.

She argued, long and determinedly, that she should break the news to Lazz herself. Heaven protect him from a logical wife. Though Marco didn't say it—he wasn't that stupid—he had no intention of allowing her anywhere near his brother without being glued to her side.

They used up precious time returning to their respective apartments to change, before driving into Dantes together. "If you'd stay in my office during my meeting with the Romanos, I'd appreciate it," he said as he worked his way through noontime traffic.

"That's okay. I'll just go to my office and—"

He released his breath in a frustrated sigh. "That wasn't a request, *cara,* despite how it may have sounded."

She stiffened. "Please tell me you're joking."

"I'm afraid not. As soon as we announce our marriage to the family, you'll be free to return to work. Until then, it would be better to keep a low profile."

"I see," she said, though he could tell that she didn't. Not even a little. "And what am I permitted to do during your meeting? Is twiddling my thumbs acceptable?"

"Perfectly acceptable. Though if you'd rather, you can phone your secretary and ask her to bring you messages or work files." Unable to resist, he leaned in and snatched a quick kiss. It relieved his mind no end when she responded to it. "Just warn her not to alert anyone to your presence."

"Like Lazz."

"Exactly."

He took them in through the back entrance, in the hopes of attracting as little attention as possible. They arrived at his office only moments before the Romanos and, after reluctantly parting from his wife, he escorted Vittorio and his daughter, Ariana, into the conference room. The meeting didn't go as well as he'd hoped. A new article had appeared just that morning in *The Snitch,* detailing how Sev had blackmailed his wife into marriage. Not quite accurate, but damning enough.

"What do you want me to do, Vittorio?" Marco finally asked. "I can't prevent them from publishing these stories. No one can. Look at the royal families in Europe. There are constant, scurrilous articles about them in the various rags. If the Royals can't put a stop to it, how can I?"

"He has a point, Papa," Ariana said.

Vittorio folded his arms across his chest and his face fell into stubborn lines. "All I hear is excuses. Maybe if you and your brothers were more circumspect, your antics wouldn't attract the attention of this rag."

Before Marco could reply, he heard Lazz's voice raised in anger from the general direction of his office. Then the door slammed open and his brother burst into the room, Caitlyn hot on his heels.

"You son of a bitch," Lazz snarled, and launched himself at Marco.

Six

Marco absorbed the impact and they hit the ground with a thud. Lazz landed several hard punches before realizing that his brother, while protecting himself, wasn't striking back.

"Fight, you bastard," Lazz shouted. "Give me an excuse to tear you apart for stealing what was mine."

Before Marco could respond, Sev and Nicolò descended on the conference room, dragging the two combatants apart. A babble of voices erupted, some in English, more in Italian. Through the mass of bodies, Marco saw Caitlyn standing off to one side, looking horrified. But even as he watched, her chin set and he could practically read her thoughts. She intended to face the ramifications of her actions, just as Marco would.

"Did you touch her?" Lazz demanded. "Did you put your hands on her?"

"Touching was unavoidable, all things considered." Marco fingered his split lip and winced. "Caitlyn and I are married."

Stunned disbelief held everyone silent for a second before all hell broke loose again. Across the room Vittorio Romano shot to his feet. Ariana began a heated argument with him but Marco could tell it wouldn't do any good. He could kiss that account goodbye. Something Ariana said must have made an impact because Vittorio hesitated and then with great reluctance pointed in Lazz's direction.

And then something very strange happened. Ariana turned to look at Lazz, whose focus remained fixed on Marco. A strange smile tilted her mouth and she nodded. "Yes, he's the one," he heard her voice in a brief lull in the shouting.

Vittorio waded through the herd of arguing Dantes to Marco's side. "Fix this," he warned. "Then call me."

Marco didn't have a clue what had just happened, but he'd take whatever fortune the gods cared to bestow and run with it. "You have my word. This will sort itself out in time."

"Make it soon," Vittorio advised.

The minute the Romanos left, Lazz swiveled in Caitlyn's direction and Marco read the determination in his brother's eyes. He leaped to his feet to put himself between the two. Sev and Nicolò moved in to block him, grabbing hold when he would have fought his way to his wife's side.

"You owe him this much," Nicolò growled.

"I don't owe him a damn thing. You don't know what he did." Unable to break free, Marco swore long and virulently. "I'm warning you, Lazz," he roared in Italian. "Stay away from my wife."

Lazz simply shot a mocking glance over his shoulder and crossed to Caitlyn's side. Marco began to fight in earnest, suspecting he knew what was to come.

"I'm sorry," he heard Caitlyn say. "I swear what happened wasn't planned."

"Not by you," Lazz agreed. "Just out of curiosity, who did you marry last night?"

She frowned in confusion. "Marco."

"Marco…or Marco posing as me?"

Her breath hitched in sudden understanding and the sight of tears glittering in her eyes nearly tore Marco apart. "Does it matter?" she asked softly. "It's done."

He hesitated a moment before nodding. "Fair enough. But, I'd still like to know. When did you know it was Marco, and not me?"

Marco stilled as his eyes locked with Caitlyn's. The fight drained from him as he waited for her to tell them all what he'd done. To betray his lies and deceit. For something fragile and unique to die before it ever had the change to gain in strength and power. He'd messed up. Badly. Broken something precious while risking the bonds of his family. And he didn't know if he could fix it. If he'd have the time to fix it.

"I knew it was Marco the instant I first set eyes on him. I immediately realized that he was the one I'd met in the lobby on my first day at Dantes." She focused on

Lazz, the expression in her eyes calm and unflinching. "Why didn't you set me straight my first day here? Why did you pretend it was you I met in the lobby?"

"I—"

She released a laugh of amused exasperation, but Marco could hear the heartache behind it. "I know. I know. You two have been competing for women since you were schoolboys."

"I'm sorry," Lazz said stiffly. "It was wrong of me. I should have told you."

A sharpness crept into her voice. "You had six weeks to correct my error. The fact that you couldn't find an appropriate occasion in all that time can only mean you deliberately kept silent in order to keep me in the dark. You also made damn certain I didn't discover you had a twin because you worried that I might question who I'd really been attracted to that day." She waved the topic aside as though it held no further importance. "Never mind. Marco and I worked it out between us. We'll consider the rest water under the bridge."

Lazz frowned. "Caitlyn, I kept silent because I didn't trust Marco to respect our relationship."

"We didn't have a relationship that first day," she said with devastating logic. "You saw an opportunity to cut your brother out of the picture and have spent weeks keeping Marco and me apart so we wouldn't catch on. Well, sorry. The game's over and you lose."

"You have every reason to be upset." He hesitated. "But Marco's joking about the two of you getting married, isn't he?"

She shook her head and summoned a brilliant smile,

one that succeeded in fooling Lazz, but didn't fool Marco in the least. She held out her left hand where her wedding rings flashed. "He wasn't kidding."

Lazz stared, stunned. "My God, Caitlyn."

"Don't." A hint of strain bled into her voice. "When it's right, it's right. That's why I was so confused while we were dating. Something happened during that first meeting with Marco, something that didn't happen in all the times you and I were together since. As soon as I met Marco, everything became clear. Just because you don't understand what my...my husband and I feel for each other, doesn't mean it doesn't exist."

Marco could see she'd reached the breaking point. This time when he fought off his brothers' hold, they released him. He crossed to Caitlyn's side and dropped an arm around her shoulders and held her close.

"Hang in there just another minute," he murmured for her ears alone. Then louder, "Caitlyn's answered all the questions she's going to. The two of us will be out for the rest of the day. Don't call unless it's urgent. And just so you know, urgent isn't on the schedule for the next twenty-four hours."

Without another word, Lazz stepped back. Sev gave an agreeable nod. "Congratulations on your marriage. Take the rest of the week if you want. We'll make sure your jobs are covered."

"Thanks." Marco answered for himself as well as Caitlyn. "We'll take it into consideration." He didn't waste another minute but escorted his wife from the building and to his car before she broke down. "We'll go to my place," he told her.

She shook her head. "I just want to go home."

"My place *is* your home," he reminded her gently. "Living apart now will make it too easy to continue living apart. That's not my idea of marriage."

"Neither is this," she whispered.

He shot her a concerned look. "Give it time. It'll get better, I promise."

She closed her eyes and leaned her head back against the seat. "You make a lot of promises, Mr. Dante."

"And I keep each and every one of them." They drew to a halt at a stoplight. "Why did you do it, Caitlyn?"

She didn't pretend to misunderstand the question. "Lazz wasn't an innocent in all this, either. In fact, a large portion of our situation can be placed squarely at his door. If he'd told me it was you in the lobby that day or warned me that he had a twin brother, last night wouldn't have happened."

Marco shrugged. "It would simply have delayed the inevitable."

She opened her eyes, eyes gone dark with painful memories. "I'd never have agreed to date you."

"You're wrong."

She considered for a moment before conceding the truth. "Okay, fine. I would have gone out with you. But as soon as I'd realized that you were—what did Britt call you?—sinfully charming, I'd have put an end to our relationship. I don't date charming."

"You married charming," he reminded her. "Besides, by the time you'd discovered just how charming I am, it would have been far too late." He put the car in gear and cruised through the intersection. "I would have won you over, just as I did last night."

When they arrived at his apartment, he took her on a brief tour. "We can shop for a new place, if you want, though this should be big enough for two. I'll let you decide."

"It's at least four times the size of my place." Impressed, she ran a hand along the back of his couch and paused to study the collage of photos on the wall, most of which were family pictures. She focused on Nonna and Primo's wedding photo. "I never did get to meet your grandparents."

"You will. Did you know they also eloped?" She shook her head and he added, "Nonna was engaged to Primo's best friend. Once The Inferno struck, that was that. There was no turning back for them, either."

Caitlyn stilled. "Is that the only reason you married me? Because of this Inferno you believe you felt?"

"We both felt The Inferno, *cara*."

Was he serious? She turned from the wall of photos to fully confront him. "Let me get this straight. The reason we're together is because of The Inferno. It has nothing to do with me? With who I am, with what type of person I am? You felt this reaction and therefore that's it. End of story. You'll marry me simply based on some family legend."

"It goes deeper than that."

"You're wrong, Marco. There isn't anything more. Nothing deeper. We felt something when we first shook hands and you assumed it was this Dante legend come to life. And all because of that, you interfered in my relationship with Lazz. You tricked me into going with you to Nevada." She fought to keep the pain and tears from her voice with only limited success. "You married me, even though you knew I thought you were your brother. And all because of a fantasy. A family superstition."

"It's not superstition. It's fact."

Anger rose to the fore. "I live by facts and figures, Marco. The Inferno is far from fact. You may believe in it. Your grandparents may believe in it. Even Sev may give it some credence, though how a man so intelligent could, is beyond me. But that doesn't make it real. That doesn't make it factual. And it's sure as hell not enough of a foundation for marriage."

"In time you'll understand."

"No, I won't, because our marriage won't last that long."

He approached with an easy, unhurried stride and slid his arms around her waist. "Let's see if I can't convince you to change your mind about that."

"What are you going to do?"

She didn't know why she bothered to ask the question. She knew precisely what he planned. It was there in his heated gaze and in his slow smile and in the tender manner in which he held her. He moved against her in a way that instantly brought their wedding night to mind, then lowered his head to coax her mouth with a single kiss.

She could feel the slight puffiness from his encounter with Lazz's fist and kept the kiss as gentle as possible, though why she felt the need for such consideration she couldn't explain. To her surprise, he didn't demand.

Didn't insist. He simply seduced with lips and teeth and tongue.

How was it possible that she surrendered with such ease after all he'd done over the past twenty-four hours? Was she so desperate to return to his bed that nothing else mattered? Where was the logic in that? How could she reconcile heart with head when every time he kissed her, her heart went wild and her head lost all ability to reason?

"Give us a chance, Caitlyn. We can make this work."

"That's not possible."

"I'll make it possible."

He swept her into his arms and shouldered his way into the bedroom. She had a brief glimpse of bright colors and gleaming woodwork before falling into the sumptuous embrace of raw silk and velvet. The handcrafted comforter cushioned her, cradling her in softness, while Marco covered her in all that was hard and male.

"This is wrong." Her hands settled on his shoulders to push, but clung instead. "I don't want you to make love to me again."

"This is even more right than last night." Urgency blazed within his eyes, sparking with green and gold lights. "When you make love to me this time, it won't just be with your husband. You'll make love to me knowing I'm Marco, not Lazz."

"So you can put your mark on me."

A hint of a smile cut through the hard edge of passion. "That happened long ago."

"You can't truly believe in this Inferno," she argued desperately. "That it's responsible for the attraction between us."

He hesitated, his hand tracing the curve of cheek and throat as though he was unwilling—or unable—to keep his hands off her. "I've been attracted to many women." His voice held a hint of apology. "But it's never been like this. I can look at you objectively and see a beautiful woman, a woman I'd want in my life and my bed."

She couldn't help stiffening against him. "And you've succeeded."

"Let me finish. I've never once wanted more from those women than a casual affair. I've never been tempted to extend our relationship beyond its temporary boundaries. But with you…" He caught her hand in his and drew it to his chest, pressed it tight to the solid beat of his heart. "With you it's as though those women were mere shadows of possibility. Shades of gray without color or substance. I don't want shadows. I want light and color. I want a woman of depth. And that's you."

"This is too much, too soon. We need time to get to know each other."

He laughed, the sound soft and deep and oddly arousing. "We have all the time in the world, *cara.* Decades to get to know every intimate detail."

"That's not what I mean—"

"I know what you mean. It's just not something I can offer you."

So compassionate, and yet so absolute. He didn't give her time to argue any further. His mouth drifted across hers, nibbling a lazy path. The casualness of the kiss should have allowed her to turn away. Instead it incited a desire to deepen it, to drive it from temperate to ardent. To feel the burn that happened only with Marco.

She whispered his name and felt him practically inhale the sound of it, felt his need as though it were her own. She expected him to exhibit some sign of victory or complacency. But he didn't. He simply gave to her, allowing her demand to set the pace.

"If I ask you to stop, will you?" she asked.

"Yes. Reluctantly. But, yes."

He needed to stop. Now. "Don't stop. Not yet. Soon—" She groaned as the buttons of her blouse gave, one by one, and he stroked his finger from the dip at the base of her throat to the scalloped edge of her bra. "Marco!"

Then his mouth followed the same path, his tongue tracing the lacy contours while he found the back fastening and released it with a flick of clever fingers. Cool air sliced across her bared skin before Marco warmed it with a single touch. He palmed her breasts and laved each tip into tight peaks, catching first one and then the other with his teeth until she could barely contain her response to the pleasure.

Her hands moved of their own accord, tearing at his shirt. She heard the cotton rip, heard the muted ping of buttons popping before she finally—*finally*—hit hot, bare flesh. Satisfaction bubbled through her like warm syrup as her hands plied the sculpted muscles, tripping across them with her fingertips. He groaned his encouragement.

She wanted more. Needed it. She cruised across rippled abs until she found the belt anchoring trousers to hips. Two deft tugs and she had it open and her hands plunging downward, cupping and stroking. Harsh

Italian exploded from him, an endless stream of what sounded like a combination of demand, curse and plea.

"Panties," she managed, praying he understood her shorthand. "Off."

Rending silk competed with the sound of their desperate breathing. And then came the pause, that long moment of sweet hesitation before temptation tipped over into inevitability. She stared up at Marco, wishing she didn't see Lazz mirrored in her husband's face and eyes, wishing that with one glance or touch or word, she could tell the difference between them. But she wasn't sure she could. Not unless she demanded he show her his hip each time they came together.

"I'm not him," Marco bit out.

"I know you're not," she attempted to soothe.

"You don't. Not yet. But you will." He fumbled behind him. She heard a drawer being yanked open and the distinctive crackle of foil. The instant he'd protected himself, he measured her length with his eyes. "Maybe this will help."

He swept his hands from her knees to her thighs, dragging her skirt upward as he went, baring her to the waist. She'd never been taken like this, simply flipped onto a bed and driven so insane with want that removing their clothes proved beyond them. She shuddered as he palmed the back of her thighs, lifting and opening her for his possession. A rush of cool air competed with the scalding heat of him as he came down on her, drove inward with a single, powerful thrust. She thought she screamed, but if she did he caught the helpless sound in a desperate kiss.

She locked her legs around his hips and surged upward to meet his next stroke, the need in her so huge and overwhelming, nothing else mattered but having this man inside her. The past didn't count anymore than the future. All she cared about was right here and right now.

Marco loosened another barrage of Italian, and she answered as though she understood, inciting him to go higher and harder and further than they'd gone before. It was her turn to plead. To demand. To pray that she survived the encounter if only so she could do this again and again.

Her climax hit with unexpected suddenness, careening through her in chaotic, unmanageable waves. No order. No logic or reason. She could only hang on and give in to something beyond her ability to control. To surrender utterly. Endless minutes passed while they fought to regain their breath.

"*Cara,* please. Don't cry."

"Am I?" She lifted a boneless hand to her cheek. "I didn't realize."

"Does it seem so wrong to you?"

No, that was the scary part. It seemed all too right. "It's just…" Damp hair curled across his brow, framing a face still carved with the remnants of desire. She itched to brush it from his eyes, and with a sigh of impatience, caved to the impulse. "It has to be more than this. More than just good sex."

He lifted an eyebrow. "Is that how you'd describe what just happened here? What happened between us last night?"

She refused to consider it might be anything else. That would give it too much importance. "There's more to a relationship than great sex," she argued doggedly. "Far more to a marriage."

"So now it's great sex," he said. "At least that's an improvement."

She slammed the heel of her palm against his shoulder, hurting herself more than him. "Would you be serious? At least with Lazz—" She broke off at the expression on his face, eyeing him apprehensively.

"Do not," he said in a low voice, "*do not* put my brother in bed with us. Not ever."

"It's just—"

"Am I not clear on this point?"

"Fine. You're clear." She shoved at his shoulders. "I'd like to get up, please."

He rolled to one side, allowing her to escape. It annoyed her that he remained so comfortable with his partial nudity, while she needed desperately to cover herself while they talked. She tugged at her wrinkled skirt, attempting to restore it to some semblance of order. Next she tackled the buttons of her blouse, only to realize she hadn't a hope of rehooking her bra unless she removed her blouse first. Turning her back on him, she did just that. A small, choking sound emanated from the direction of the bed and sounded suspiciously like a smothered laugh, though when she turned back around he regarded her with such a sober expression that it stretched the bounds of credulity.

She decided to give him the benefit of the doubt. "I'm a logical person, Marco," she finally said. "And though I enjoy sex as much as the next person—"

"Great sex," he reminded her.

"Fine. *Great* sex." He'd thrown her off track and it took a split second to find her stride again. "Marriage is more than sex. Even great sex," she hastened to add before he could correct her again.

"True," he surprised her by saying. "Since we have that part down pat, we can spend the next fifty or so years working on the rest." He lifted an eyebrow. "Does that alleviate your concerns, *moglie mia?*"

Caitlyn planted her hands on her hips. "Why do you use so much Italian? Lazz never—" She broke off and rubbed the exhaustion from her eyes. He was right, Lazz didn't belong in the room with them. "I'm sorry. I meant to say that you use a lot of Italian and I don't understand a word of it. What does mog-whatever mean?"

Marco left the bed. "*Moglie* means wife." After stripping off the remains of his tattered shirt, he disappeared into the adjoining bathroom. When he reappeared, he paused in front of her and dropped a swift kiss on her brow. "Thank you for trying."

She didn't dare admit that Lazz might as well not have existed right then, despite her reference to him. Not while Marco stood in front of her, shirtless, his trousers gaping at the waist where a thin line of dark hair darted downward along a path she'd just recently followed. She struggled to keep her gaze fixed on his face. He must have known how difficult she found it not to peek, because a slow grin built across his mouth.

"I'm your husband, remember?" he said. "We have a piece of paper that says it's not rude to look."

"I must have missed that particular line on our marriage license," she muttered.

"Ah. That's because you forgot your reading glasses."

She lifted an eyebrow. "And if I'd remembered them?"

He shrugged those magnificent shoulders of his. "Fate and chance give life interesting twists and turns, wouldn't you agree?"

"Since I'm currently in a twist over one of those wrong turns, I'm not sure *interesting* is the word I'd use."

He fell silent for a moment. "I don't consider our marriage a wrong turn," he informed her quietly. "In time I hope you won't, either."

She'd been inconsiderate, and hurt him without meaning to. It occurred to her that in the short time they'd been together, he'd used great care with her. Despite some of his more outrageous actions, everything he'd said, as well as his overall treatment of her, had been not just careful but downright tender. The least she could do was follow his example.

"Where are we supposed to go from here?" she asked.

"I was thinking the kitchen might be a good direction."

She stared at him in patent disbelief. "You want me to cook for you?"

Lord help her, but Marco liked to laugh. "Actually, I thought I'd cook for you."

After snagging a shirt, he ushered her into the kitchen and seated her at a tiny table tucked within the sunny embrace of a bay window. Opening a drawer, he removed an apron, which he tied around his waist with such familiarity and efficiency, she realized this was far from his first foray into the kitchen. Coffee came first, freshly ground. And then he proceeded to cook. Really cook. In less than thirty minutes he placed two steaming plates of shrimp fettuccini on the table. After whipping off his apron, he joined her.

"If this is to impress me…"

"Has it succeeded?"

"And then some." She sampled the dish and groaned. "Do you cook like this all the time?"

"When I'm not out of the country or entertaining potential clients. I got lucky and found a woman to shop for me who appreciates fine food as much as I do. I e-mail her when I want something to appear in my refrigerator." He shrugged. "And it appears. She also takes care of general housekeeping and various other chores that don't appeal to me as much as cooking."

For some reason, that had Caitlyn returning her fork to her plate. "Maybe this would be a good time to discuss our marriage."

He picked up her fork and speared a succulent piece of shrimp and held it to her mouth. "Fine. What, in particular, would you like to discuss?"

"Marco…" She couldn't resist. She ate the shrimp, took the fork from him and dug in again. "What do you want from our marriage?"

"Ah. You'd like rules. Order."

"I'd like some idea of your expectations."

"Scintillating conversation and companionship. Incredible sex—we'll have to work to nudge it up from great. And with God's blessing, more laughter than tears." He lifted an eyebrow. "I can go on. Do you want me to fetch your PDA so you can jot down some notes?"

"I need you to be serious. Marriage is a serious business." Her fork clattered to her plate. An empty plate, she realized to her amazement. "I'm sorry. I just can't do this. None of this is real and it's pointless to pretend otherwise."

"Marriage is not a business and I refuse to turn it into one." He reached across the table and caught her hand. "Relax, *cara.* You need to give our relationship time and stop applying an agenda to it. Do flowers bloom on command? Does spring arrive simply because the calendar says it must? If it makes you more comfortable to create some sense of order, then let's call this moment in our marriage point A. In a few weeks we can reassess and see if we haven't moved to B or C."

For some reason that had her eyes filling. "This is crazy, you know that, don't you?"

"Tears," he said with a frown. "Now that I will keep track of. Because for every tear, I'm going to make certain you have reason to laugh at least a hundred times."

"At this rate I'm going to spend all day laughing."

"See how easy that was? We already have our first marital rule. A hundred laughs for every tear." The humor in his gaze eased, replaced by undisguised warmth. "I know you planned to tell me today that you're leaving and putting an end to our marriage. But will you agree to stay and give it a try? We can set a time frame if that makes you more comfortable."

"A negotiation, Marco?"

"I could, if I considered marriage a business deal. I could use *The Snitch* as an excuse or the Romano account."

She stirred uneasily. "Will our marriage have an adverse impact on that?"

"No. But our divorce would." He let that settle for a minute before continuing. "I could explain how much more beneficial it would be to your career to remain with me, or how it would look if we divorced after a single day of marriage. But this isn't about business, as I've already explained. There's only one real reason to stay together."

"Which is…what?" She hazarded a guess. "To get to point Z?"

He smiled, a gorgeous, sexy smile that she'd never ever seen on Lazz Dante's face. Only Marco could smile like that. "Why would I want to jump straight to Z when there are so many fun points to explore in between? The point of a dance is not to rush to the end, but to enjoy each step along the way." He pulled her up from her chair and swung her into his arms, causing her to melt helplessly against him. "Come, my beautiful wife. What do you say? Let's dance."

Seven

Over the next few days, Caitlyn discovered that Marco meant just what he said. He didn't seem to care about the business ramifications should she walk out on him. He only cared about her. For some reason, that realization left her shaken. All the while a small voice whispered insistently in her ear that it had to be a lie. How could she possibly be more important than winning an account that would guarantee the meteoric success of Dantes in the European market?

Marriage should be more complicated than Marco was making it out to be. It certainly had been for her grandmother. Thanks to her disastrous union, there'd been exhaustive instructions on how to build a proper foundation and which qualities to look for in a husband, an endless list to be detailed, considered and checked off long before marriage should ever be contemplated. She and Marco hadn't done any of that, and Caitlyn couldn't help but believe that lack would bring a fast end to a short marriage.

Fortunately, she didn't have long to dwell on her worries. The minute she returned to work, she was assigned a huge, complex project to oversee that involved transferring decades worth of old financial records from paper to computer.

"With the expansion into the international market, we need to have this information available at the touch of a button," Caitlyn's supervisor explained. "And we need someone with your background in finance and attention to detail to sort the wheat from the chaff. Determine what's important to computerize and what can be safely discarded."

"But what about my current duties?"

"We're assigning you temporary help with that while you concentrate on getting this other project in hand. I'll be honest with you, Caitlyn. We're hoping you can succeed where every other person who's attempted this assignment has failed."

It was like waving a red flag in front of a bull, Caitlyn realized with a touch of Marco's sense of humor. The idea that she could accomplish what no one else had appealed immensely and she threw herself into the project with un-fettered enthusiasm. Unfortunately, it meant a temporary move from the Dantes main office to their warehouse where most of the records were stored.

Toward the end of the week, Britt tracked Caitlyn down at her new location and tossed a folder onto her desk. "Here. Lazz said you needed this. I could have e-mailed it to you, but it gave me an excuse to come for a visit. Just so you know, you're missed."

"Thanks. I miss you and Angie, too." She checked her watch. "I wish I'd known you were coming. I'm actually scheduled to have lunch with Francesca in about five minutes."

"Sev's wife, right?" Britt grimaced. "Makes sense. I guess she's been assigned to explain what the family will expect from the latest Dante bride."

Caitlyn's brows drew together. "Expect? What are you talking about?"

Britt snapped her fingers. "Oh, come on, girl. Get with it. You're in the public eye now. *The Snitch* will be all over you when news of your whirlwind marriage to Marco breaks. I suspect Primo or Nonna assigned Francesca as your handler, to guide you through the various family dos and don'ts so you don't accidentally make matters worse for them than you already have."

It took an instant before Caitlyn could gather herself enough to reply. "I'm sure that's not the case at all."

Britt shrugged. "If you say so." She shoved a pile of papers to one side and levered herself onto the desktop. Lifting Caitlyn's left hand, she let out a low whistle. "That's one hell of a rock, sweetie. Even more impressive than the one Lazz was planning to give you."

Caitlyn tugged her hand free, annoyed at the hint of color she felt creeping into her cheeks, and even more annoyed at Britt. "You and Angie made a bigger deal of my relationship with Lazz than it warranted."

"Apparently. Poor Lazz. I guess you fell for Marco's

charm just like every other woman working at Dantes." She leaned in, lowering her voice. "So is it true?"

"Is what true?" But Caitlyn could guess, given the various rumors flying around the office about the events that had transpired the night she and Marco had eloped.

A wicked light gleamed in her friend's eyes. "Did you realize it was Marco before he made love to you, or did he wait until afterward to tell you the truth?"

Even though Caitlyn had seen the question coming, she still winced. "I should have expected something like that from you, but you must realize I'm not going to answer it."

Britt blew out a sigh. "Or which of the two is the better lover?" She paused a beat, but when Caitlyn remained stony silent, added, "It's gotta be Marco. I mean, why else would you marry him, especially considering that jealous streak of his?"

"Caitlyn?" Francesca's voice came from a short distance away.

"Oops. That's my cue to scoot." Britt jumped off Caitlyn's desk and waggled her fingers. "We'll catch up again later."

Francesca, tall, blond and as elegant as she was beautiful, appeared in the doorway. She waited with ill-disguised disapproval while Britt made good her escape. "Come on, let's get out of here," she said to Caitlyn. "I don't know about you, but I could use some fresh air."

"Where are we going?"

"To Nonna's so she can explain how you're expected to behave now that you're a Dante bride." She waved the comment aside with a broad grin. "Sorry. I couldn't resist. We are going to Nonna's for lunch, but I assure you if there's a Dante bride how-to instruction booklet somewhere, Britt will have to show it to me. To be honest, there are times I could really use one."

On the way to Francesca's car, Caitlyn attempted to defend her friend, though why she bothered, she couldn't say. "Britt's just a bit outspoken."

"Is that what you call it? I call it pea green with envy." Slipping the car in gear, Francesca pulled out of the parking lot and jumped on the 101 toward the Golden Gate Bridge. "She's always had a thing for Marco. But he and his brothers made an agreement years ago that they wouldn't date in the workplace. Of course, that agreement fell apart when I came onboard."

"Did that count? I thought you were dating Sev before you joined Dantes."

"Was blackmailed into joining Dantes. Don't you read *The Snitch?* I guess Britt saw my relationship with Sev as a loosening of the rule and made a concerted effort to catch Marco's eye. Then when both Lazz and Marco went after you…" Francesca shrugged. "I'm sure it felt like a slap in the face to poor Britt."

Caitlyn considered the situation. Sunlight poured down across the red spans of the bridge and bounced off the whitecaps far below. If Francesca's comments were accurate, it explained many of the barbed remarks Britt claimed were jokes. "Thanks, Francesca. I appreciate you clueing me in."

Sympathy gleamed in Francesca's dark eyes. "Anytime. I'm just sorry I had to trash someone you consider a friend."

Caitlyn leaned back against her seat and studied her sister-in-law for a long minute. How odd that with one simple "I do" she'd gone from having almost no family to having one so sizeable that she didn't even know all their names or faces yet.

A few minutes later they climbed the hillside above Sausalito and pulled into the drive of a large, rambling gated home. Francesca led the way through the dusky interior and out into a huge, meticulously tended garden, overrun with flowers, shrubs and shade trees. A wrought iron table had been placed beneath the widespread arms of a mush oak and set for lunch. Seated at the table was a woman who could only be Nonna.

Caitlyn returned the older woman's stare, fascinated by Marco's grandmother. She must be well into her seventies, considering she and Primo just celebrated their fifty-sixth anniversary. Yet she looked a full decade younger, her face one of radiant beauty despite the lines life had carved there. Or maybe because of them.

"Marco has your eyes," Caitlyn observed.

Laughter danced within the hazel depths, revealing that Marco had inherited a second characteristic from his grandmother. "So does Lazzaro," she said, her voice carrying the lilting strains of her Italian heritage. "Or did you not notice?"

Caitlyn blinked in surprise. "I…I guess I never did. But, of course they would since they're identical twins."

Nonna lifted a shoulder. "Ah. Once you have been touched by The Inferno, you see only one man clearly." She kissed Caitlyn on both cheeks, followed by Francesca, then gestured to the two empty chairs. "Come. Sit. You will call me Nonna as Francesca does, and we will break bread together and talk as women have talked since the day we were formed from Adam's rib. About men, life, children and then, inevitably, about men again."

Francesca grinned. "Sounds good to me. Especially the men part."

"Hah. With you I suspect children are more on your thoughts, yes?"

"Not quite yet, Nonna."

"Time will tell. I am rarely wrong about these matters. But since that is not yet an issue, we will have a lovely glass of wine with our lunch." A mischievous expression twinkled in her eyes. "Maybe two."

"I'm sorry, Nonna," Caitlyn began. "I can't—"

"Because you are not finished with your workday." Nonna waved that aside and poured the wine. "If it makes you more comfortable, consider keeping me happy for the rest of the day one of your duties. One of your primary duties since I have arranged for you to have the afternoon off. And keeping me happy right now involves drinking some Dante wine while we get to know each other."

Caitlyn gave in gracefully. "A dangerous proposition. Last time I had a glass of your Dante wine, I ended up married to Marco."

The other two women dissolved into laughter. "Such is The Inferno," Nonna said. "It turns sane, rational women into creatures of instinct."

The comment roused Caitlyn's curiosity. "Would you mind if I asked you both a personal question?"

"Hit me," Francesca said.

Nonna looked momentarily disconcerted at the response but nodded energetically, anyway. "Yes, yes. You may hit me, too. But I am old, so do it very gently."

"It's more of a verbal hit," Caitlyn explained with a smile. "I know you believe in The Inferno, Nonna. Marco told me how it changed your life and forced you to make a difficult choice."

"Not so difficult. More sad and unpleasant."

Caitlyn glanced at her sister-in-law. "But you, Francesca. Do you believe in it?"

Francesca relaxed in her chair and took a sip of the crisp, golden Frascati. "I gather you don't?"

Caitlyn shook her head. "I think it must be legend or fantasy," she said, shooting Nonna an apologetic look.

"Yes, so did I. At first. It's only natural, all things considered."

"You said...at first. That implies that at some point you bought in to the story."

Instead of laughing, an odd expression settled over Francesca's face. "Give me an honest answer, Caitlyn. Was there an electric current when you and Marco first touched? I mean, an honest-to-goodness spark?"

"There was something like that," she admitted.

"And do you feel him, even when you don't see him? If I lined up Lazz and Marco in identical suits. If I mixed them up and turned them so their backs were to you. Could you tell which was your husband and which your brother-in-law?"

"I'm not sure." Perhaps if she could look directly at them, catch some clue as to expression or attitude. Or would it take that much effort? The mere idea of Lazz putting his hands on her struck her as downright distasteful. She closed her eyes. "I honestly don't know. Maybe."

"Does Marco rub his palm, like this?" Francesca demonstrated, digging the fingers of her left hand into the center of her right. "Look familiar?"

"Yes," Caitlyn whispered. "I've caught him doing it on occasion. I catch myself doing it, too."

"It happens with all the Dante men once they have been struck by The Inferno, and it would seem, with some of the Dante brides," Nonna explained. "Primo. Our two sons. And now Sev and Marco. So it has been since the beginning of the Dante line."

"It's up to you whether or not you choose to believe that it's The Inferno." Francesca shrugged. "I happen to believe."

Before Caitlyn could ask more questions, Primo delivered their lunch, one he'd prepared for them himself. Clearly, Marco had inherited Primo's ability in the kitchen, despite there being more of a physical resemblance between the older man and Sev. Though Primo's countenance reflected an almost harsh nobility, only warmth showed in his expression. After welcoming her with a warm bear hug and a smacking kiss on each cheek, he checked to see whether they had everything they needed, then made himself scarce.

The hours raced by after that, brimming with sweet, tart laughter and rich, full-bodied feminine conversation. Caitlyn couldn't remember ever having a more enjoyable time in the company of women. At one point she attempted to compare Nonna with her own grandmother, but aside from a certain strength of character, the two couldn't be more dissimilar.

Early evening had just crept into the garden, pinching shut colorful day blooms and coaxing open their heavy-scented nocturnal sisters, when the Dante boys descended. Sev took one look at his wife and shook his head in mock dismay. "I see Nonna's been a bit heavy-handed with the wine," he addressed his grandfather. "I'm going to need your wheelbarrow to get this one home."

"You know where I stash it," Primo said with a chuckle. He pulled a chair up beside Nonna and gathered her hand in his. Heads bent toward each other like a pair of sleepy white daffodils and they murmured softly in Italian.

Caitlyn sensed Marco's approach and knew that Francesca and Nonna would claim it was The Inferno at work. Whatever caused the awareness, it mitigated her surprise when he simply picked her up in his arms, stole her seat, then sat down again with her on his lap.

"How was your day?" he asked.

"Perfect." Her head dropped of its own accord to his shoulder. "Better than perfect."

"I'm glad. Nonna is…" He shrugged.

"There's no describing her, is there?" Caitlyn agreed.

They continued to sit, the six of them, and talk for another hour before Marco called it a night. They made their farewells and exited through the garden gate to the circular drive, maintaining a comfortable silence on the drive from Sausalito to Marco's apartment.

"Nonna's different from my grandmother," Caitlyn commented on their way inside.

"You know, I think that's the first time you've mentioned your family since our wedding night." He inclined his head toward the rear of the apartment. "Fill me in while we change. How's your grandmother different from mine?"

She followed him into the bedroom and stripped off her suit jacket. "They're both strong women," she said, heading for the closet. "But Gran was rigid. Nonna... not so much."

He reached around her for a wooden hanger. "Let me guess. Your grandmother came from the school of thought that teaches seeing is believing." He nudged her with his elbow. "Passed that right on to you, did she?"

A smile flirted with Caitlyn's mouth, then faded. "She didn't have much choice. She raised me, you know. Or maybe you don't know." She shot him an uneasy glance. "Sorry. I guess it was Lazz I told."

To her relief, he didn't take offense. "Tell me now," he encouraged. He unzipped her skirt for her, before ripping free his tie with a sigh of relief.

She stepped out of her skirt and clipped it to the hanger holding her suit jacket. It never ceased to amaze her how comfortable she felt performing these little domestic chores in front of him. Relishing the sizzle of awareness combined with the gentle bite of sexual tension. Wondering if the sight of her half-undressed would tempt him to pick her up and toss her to the bed behind them. If his nudity would tempt her to entice him there. She suddenly realized he was waiting for her response.

"Oh, it's an old, sad story," she hastened to explain.

"One told by countless women over the years. My grandfather was a charmer."

She broke off when Marco lassoed her with his tie and yanked her up against him. "Excuse me?" he rumbled.

She couldn't help but grin. "Oh, stop glaring at me. I don't mean your kind of charmer."

"What other kind is there?" he asked, genuinely bewildered.

Her amusement evaporated. "The sort who makes pie-in-the-sky promises and neglects to keep them." She strained against the confines of the tie, regarding him with amused exasperation. "Do you mind?"

"Another time, perhaps." He reluctantly released her and continued to undress. "That explains why my promises worry you so much. You don't know me well enough to believe I'll keep them."

"Something like that," she confessed. "Gramps encouraged Gran to give up a high-powered budding career, which in those days, very few women managed to achieve. But she did it because he sold her on the dream."

He leaned against the closet doorjamb, shirtless, his only covering a black pair of boxer briefs. "Which was?" he prompted.

She tore her gaze away and scrambled to remember where she'd left off in her story. "He…he wanted the dream. A two-story home and white picket fence, dinner on the table at six, where a freckle-faced son with a slingshot tucked in his back pocket would be waiting for him, along with a sweet little daddy's girl dressed in a frilly dress and pigtails."

"What did he end up with?"

"A ramshackle house in dire need of repair with a fence falling into splinters, a dinner of mac and cheese because the budget didn't stretch to more than that, and a squalling daughter suffering from colic. Somehow it managed to escape his attention that in order to have the dream, someone had to earn a living. Not long after my mother was born, he took off. He'd found a new dream that appealed far more than the realities of the old one."

"What happened to your grandmother and mother?"

She turned to face him. "Gran raised my mother the best she could. Worked whatever menial jobs she managed to pick up, since by then the possibility of a career had passed her by. My mother took off at sixteen with the first man who looked twice at her. I landed on Gran's doorstep nine months later."

"Hell, sweetheart." He wrapped her up in a hug. "Saying I'm sorry sounds so inadequate. But I am."

Caitlyn shrugged, inhaling the unique scent of him. God, he smelled good, and felt even better—strength and warmth and comfort all rolled into one. "I had Gran. And my mother showed up periodically, whenever she found herself between boyfriends. Then the next rainbow would appear in the sky and she'd go dashing after it, certain that this time she'd luck into that pot of gold. Took after my grandfather, Gran always said. It's been years since I last saw her."

"And your grandmother?"

"She died of Alzheimer's a few years ago. She'd talk about him sometimes. Gramps. She didn't have a clue who I was, but she'd talk about when Jimmy came back, how they'd have the dream. Maybe it's good that her disease offered her some happiness at the end. I don't think she experienced much all the years I knew her."

He pulled back an inch to gaze down at her. "You have the Dantes now, *cara*." Emotion gave his voice a musical lilt. "You know that, right? No matter what anyone says about our marriage, we look after our own."

His comment reminded her of her run-in with Britt. "Would you mind if I asked you a question about your past?" she said hesitantly. "You don't have to answer. It's just…"

He winced. "Uh-oh. Busted. Who, what, when and why?"

"Britt stopped by my office today right before Francesca arrived to take me to lunch."

His expression gave nothing away. "And?"

"Francesca mentioned that Britt once hit on you." Caitlyn struggled to keep her voice casual. Not that she succeeded in fooling him. "Did she? Hit on you, I mean?"

He released a rough sigh. "I'd call it more of a tap than an actual hit, one I politely ignored."

A swift smile came and went. "Mr. Irresistible," she managed to tease.

He gave a short, ironic laugh. "I'll take your word for it. Some women hit on me, though whether it's because I'm irresistible or not I can't say. More irresistible for most women is that I'm a Dante and they want the sparkle a Dante husband can bring to a marriage. After all these years, I can tell the difference. Britt likes the sparkle."

"While I prefer the spark."

"So I've noticed." He slid a hand around the nape of

Caitlyn's neck and lifted her for a lingering kiss. "My turn to ask a question."

She wrinkled her nose. "Who, what, when and why?"

"Why did Francesca feel the need to tell you about Britt?"

Once again Caitlyn tried for casual and once again came up short. "Britt demonstrated a bit too much curiosity about how I ended up with you instead of Lazz."

"It was more than that, wasn't it?" When she didn't respond, he let it go. "You're a loyal friend, Caitlyn. But you have nothing to worry about when it comes to other women. Once The Inferno strikes, that's it. No one else exists as far as I'm concerned."

"Prove it."

The words slipped out before she could stop them, and his response came in a flash. Determination hardened his features and he kissed her with a passion that instantly sent her spinning out of control. Over the past several days he'd gained a familiarity with how to arouse her, how to drive her soaring to the highest peaks. Of course, it didn't take much. A kiss. A touch. Even a look seemed to ignite the flame between them.

Their remaining few clothes slid away with soft sighs, forming a path of cotton and silk from closet to bed. Where had her anger gone these past days? Her indignation over his deception? They'd both vanished in the face of a far more powerful emotion, one that left her mindless with need, a need only one man could fulfill.

Gran would have called her every kind of fool for putting fantasy ahead of reality. But in that moment Caitlyn didn't care. Winding her arms around her husband, she surrendered, soaring over rainbows and floating away on clouds of pleasure. Tomorrow would have to take care of itself.

Tonight she'd take the dream.

Eight

She was gone.

Marco came instantly awake. He didn't try to explain this new awareness of Caitlyn's presence or absence, but simply tossed back the covers to go in search of his wife. He tracked her down raiding the refrigerator. To his amusement, she'd prepared a snack for two.

"I see by all those sandwiches that you knew I'd come," he said with a yawn.

"Yes." He caught a hint of resignation in her voice. "No doubt you'll say it's The Inferno."

He took the plate from her and set it aside. Wrapping his arms around her, he rested his forehead against hers. "It still bothers you, doesn't it?"

"Yes."

Simple and concise and down-to-the-bones honest.

He appreciated that about her. "Do you think The Inferno makes what we feel for each other less real?" he asked.

Despite the lack of light, he could see her gaze grow troubled. "If our relationship is all at the whim of this Inferno, then it isn't because of who I am as a person. Or who you are, for that matter. We're just mated to each other without anything in common other than sexual attraction. How long do you think that's going to last?"

"Got it." He cut straight to the heart of the matter. "You want security. You want assurances. You want to know that we're still going to be together fifty years from now."

She choked on a laugh that contained more than a hint of tears. "I'll take a year, for now. Even a week. But I keep waiting for the other shoe to drop. For it to all go horribly wrong. If what we feel is due to The Inferno, then it's fantasy, not reality."

"It's more than that, Caitlyn, and you know it." He leaned back against the kitchen counter and cushioned her against his chest. "Either The Inferno is real or it's fantasy. If it's fantasy, it'll end and you'll get hurt. But if it's real, you're afraid your ability to make your own choices in life will be taken out of your control."

Caitlyn nodded. "What if we decide we don't like each other? What if we aren't able to build a lasting foundation together? What if we discover that our goals in life are entirely different? According to you, we're trapped together forever."

Okay, that hurt. "Do you feel trapped, *cara?*"

"Sometimes," she confessed.

He cupped her face and kissed her, imbuing it with as much tenderness and reassurance as he could. "I suspect that's true of all love, not just with The Inferno. You haven't lost a piece of yourself. You've gained something you didn't have before. At least, I have."

Instead of relaxing, her frown deepened. "But when The Inferno happened, didn't you feel as though you'd lost all control?"

"Of course. And I understand you feel the need to direct your own life." He shrugged. "I have no intention of interfering with that."

"You already have," she pointed out softly.

A hint of impatience colored his words. "Honey, no one has total control over their lives and most have only limited self-direction. Control is the illusion, self-direction the fantasy."

"It's my illusion and my fantasy, just as The Inferno is yours," she insisted stubbornly.

"You refuse to believe it might exist because of your grandmother." He could see he was treading on dangerous ground, but no longer cared. "Your bedtime story may have been a cautionary one of lost dreams. Mine was more along the lines of 'The Big Bad Wolf.' You know, the one with all those annoying little pigs."

A brief smile flirted with her mouth, a mouth he'd practically ravaged only hours earlier. "I believe that was 'The Three Little Pigs.'"

"Yeah, well, at the tender age of three, I was a bloodthirsty little savage and cheering for the wolf. The point is, I'm well aware that if we build our foundation with straw that it will get blown away. Or we can build it with stone so it withstands the fiercest storms. We choose the tools and materials. We also choose our dreams. Together."

"You make it sound so simple." She hesitated and he could practically see her organizing her little list of ifs, ands and buts. "This obsession of yours isn't logical, Marco. I don't understand why you're so dead set on believing in a fairy tale. So set that you'd marry a woman you only knew for five minutes."

His mouth tightened and a hint of old pain came and went in his eyes. "My parents were excellent examples of the worst a marriage can be, just as Primo and Nonna were excellent examples of the best. My grandparents heeded The Inferno when it struck, and their marriage is fast approaching six decades. My father ignored it, and he never knew a happy day in all his married life."

Her eyes widened in shock. "You're kidding. I assumed... Your mother wasn't—"

He shook his head. "Dad's Inferno bride, no. She was a business transaction. Despite Primo's warnings, my father married my mother for the good of Dantes, though even that didn't turn out the way either of my parents planned." He had to make her understand. "You may think it's superstition or fantasy. But I lived with the reality. I'll take anything else over that."

"Oh, Marco. I'm so sorry."

He could see the lingering doubt, could tell that she thought his actions in marrying her were an overreaction. "Listen to me, *cara*. If I hadn't made the choice I did, if I hadn't swept you off to Nevada and married you, Lazz would have eventually found a rational argument to convince you to marry him. The only person I've ever met more logical than you is him." She started to interrupt and he cut her off. "If you hadn't married me, if you'd married my brother instead, it wouldn't have just been the two of us who'd have suffered, but Lazz and his future wife, as well. He may not thank me for what I did right now, but that will change when he experiences The Inferno for himself."

She shook her head in wonder. "You really believe this."

"I do." He held her gaze. "And before long, so will you. I don't care how long it takes, or what I have to do to convince you, eventually you'll believe in The Inferno."

For the first time since they'd been married, Caitlyn arrived at the apartment without Marco. He had a meeting with Nicolò that he'd warned might run late, and sure enough, it had. She changed into jeans and a tee, then wandered restlessly through the apartment. It had an uncomfortably empty feel. She'd never realized how much her husband filled it up with his personality until he wasn't there.

There were signs of her presence around the place now, bits and pieces that Marco had plucked from her apartment and scattered about his. He hadn't pressured her to give up her old lease. At least, not yet. And she appreciated his patience. But little by little her apartment became emptier and emptier while his became fuller and more complete.

Most interesting of all, her personal treasures had found places here, places where they fit and meshed. Her grandmother's silver tea service gleamed proudly atop Marco's chiffonier in the dining room. Her collection of blown glass knickknacks glittered softly along the fireplace mantel. Her mysteries competed with his science fiction books. And their clothes, which had started out rigidly organized into proper his-and-hers sides of the closet had somehow met in the middle and mated into a colorful collection of "theirs."

She glanced at the box of files she'd brought home and stretched out on the couch with a sigh. Might as well get to work. Maneuvering the box onto the endmost couch cushion by her feet, she perched her reading glasses on the tip of her nose and pulled out the first stack of files.

She'd found a number of confusing records buried among the personal papers and wanted to take her time and sort through them in order to determine how best to handle the information they contained. Before she could do more than flip open the first folder, she heard Marco's key in the lock.

There was a confusingly long pause. Then, *"Cara?"*

She couldn't stop a smile from spreading across her face. "In here."

He appeared in the archway between the living room and hallway, a briefcase in one hand, a newspaper in the other. She could tell from his face that something was wrong and sat up.

"What's happened?"

"Damn rag. I found it shoved under our door." He tossed it to her. "Let me warn you, you're not going to like it."

That explained what had slowed him at the door. She adjusted her glasses and the newsprint swam into focus. *Marital mix-up...Marco or Lazz? Confused bride is tricked at the altar.* With an exclamation of fury, she ripped through the pages to the article the front teaser had alluded to. "My God, Marco, they know. It's all here. That I was dating Lazz first. That I met you and you pretended to be your brother. How we ran off to Nevada for a spur-of-the-moment marriage. The fight. They've chronicled every last detail."

"Not every detail, I hope."

Delicate color washed across her cheekbones, though whether from anger or embarrassment, she couldn't have said for certain. "No, not every detail. But close enough. When did this come out? I wonder if it's what set Britt off. It would certainly explain a lot."

"It's possible, though I doubt Britt needs anything specific to set her off." He joined Caitlyn on the couch and unceremoniously dumped the box of files onto the floor. Stretching out his legs in front of him, he leaned against the back cushion and loosened his tie. "Something's bothering me about these articles and I haven't quite put my finger on what it is."

"You mean something more than the articles themselves?"

"Yeah." He scooped up her legs and pulled them across his lap. His large hands closed over her sock-covered feet and began to absentmindedly knead the narrow arch. "This last month or so they've changed in tenor."

Ever since that night on the plane he'd continued his habit of massaging her feet, something that never failed to drive her straight up the wall. She stretched like a cat, sending the stack of files cascading off her lap and scattering across the hardwood floor. Marco started to get up to rescue them and she planted her toes against his rock-hard abs and pushed him back down. No way was he going anywhere anytime soon.

"Forget the files. I'll get them later. Tell me how the articles have changed. What's different about them?"

He subsided against the cushions. "They've gotten personal. Vindictive. You know…" His brow creased in thought. "I think that's it. I mean, before, they'd write up some chatty little piece about a party we'd attended, who we were dating. Every once in a while there'd be a slight hiss or meow behind the captions. But nothing damaging."

"It's sure damaging now. It's gotten downright personal."

"That's exactly what's bothering me. It is personal. And damn specific." His frown deepened. "Too specific, now that I think about it. Whoever's writing these articles must have a mole working at Dantes. It's the only explanation."

"You must be kidding."

Marco shook his head, smiling a bit at her shock. "It's not unheard of. And it's not like we have our employees sign a confidentiality agreement regarding the family's personal life."

"Maybe you should start."

"I'll mention it to Sev. Get legal on it. In the meantime, if we can find the person passing on the information, we can cut off *The Snitch*'s source and salvage the Romano account."

Oh, dear. "Have we lost it?"

"I like the way you say 'we.'" He reached out a long arm and snagged the neckline of her tee, pulling her in for a lingering kiss. "And no, *we* haven't lost the account. Yet. I warned them this would come out. Too many people overheard the commotion when we returned to Dantes the morning after our wedding for it not to have hit *The Snitch*. But the very fact that the fight is detailed so precisely in the article is evidence that the rag has an internal source of information."

"What I don't understand is why it's such a big deal for the Romanos if the Dantes are featured in this thing." She balled up the newspaper and tossed it toward the fireplace. "I'm serious, Marco. Why does it matter what a stateside rag prints about you and your family? It can't have that serious an impact on the Romanos."

Marco shrugged. "They have a reputation to protect. According to Vittorio, scandal doesn't touch the Romanos. Nor does it touch the Romanos' associates, or they're no longer associated."

"Huh. That seems a bit over the top." She lifted an eyebrow. "Doesn't his reaction strike you as excessive?"

"That's Vittorio for you. He's ferocious when it comes to guarding the Romano name and I gather he doesn't want *The Snitch* turning its investigative light on him."

"Makes sense." She gave it a moment's consideration. "I guess a family that old must have a lot of skeletons they'd rather not have uncovered, especially if they're publicity shy."

"Let's just hope to God they don't find out about The Inferno. We consider the Inferno intensely private. No one knows about it, except family, and we intend to keep it that way." Marco rolled onto his hip to face her. "Let's forget about the Romanos. And *The Snitch*'s snitch. And everything Dantes. There's only one thing I care about right now."

She couldn't help grinning. "And what would that be, Mr. Dante?" she asked, all wide-eyed innocence.

He maneuvered on top of her and plastered every foot of hard male body over every inch of hers, pressing her deep into the soft cushions. He plucked her glasses off the end of her nose and carefully set them aside. "I'm sure we'll come up with something."

It wasn't until hours later that they drifted from couch to bed. Their clothes had long since disappeared into the jumble of files and documents papering the floor. And Caitlyn simply left them there, something that would have been unheard of a few short weeks ago.

The next morning was a different story and she zipped around, gathering up the papers while Marco rescued their clothing. She didn't bother sorting or organizing—something else unheard of only weeks before—but dumped everything haphazardly into the box. She reached for a final stapled document when Lazz's name, coupled with the Romanos', practically jumped off the page. She scanned swiftly, aware that if they didn't leave soon they'd both be late for work. But what she read had her rocking back on her heels.

"What is it?" Marco asked. "What's the holdup?"

"Nothing." She shoved the document into the box and tamped down the lid. "Let's go."

"Seriously, what is it?"

She avoided his gaze and retrieved her purse and briefcase. "Just a document I need to read more carefully. I can do that when we get to work." All business now, she gestured toward the box. "Would you mind carrying it out to the car for me?"

To her relief, the moment passed. The instant Marco dropped her off at the warehouse, she made a beeline for her temporary office and ripped off the lid of the box. She snatched up the document and read it three times before she could convince herself that it was authentic. A second document followed the first, this one in Italian. But she suspected it said the exact same thing as the English version.

She didn't waste any further time. After concealing the document within the protective cover of a file folder, she called for a cab to take her to Dantes' corporate building and, once there, waited impatiently for the elevator to sweep her up to the finance department. Britt sat in the small reception area just outside Lazz's office, and Caitlyn hesitated. She'd forgotten she'd have to go through Britt to get to Lazz.

Caitlyn clutched the file against her chest. "Is he free?" she asked, striving for casual and breezy.

"Change your mind already?" Britt asked with a laugh. "Poor Marco."

"Seriously, Britt. It's important and I'm short on time."

Her friend's expression cooled. "I'm sorry, Mrs. Dante. I didn't mean to keep you waiting. I'll see if Lazz is available." She picked up the phone and hit a button. "Your sister-in-law is here to see you. No, Marco's wife. She claims it's urgent. Certainly. I'll send her right in."

The second she hung up the phone, Caitlyn tried again. "Look, I'm sorry. It's just that this is rather urgent. I didn't mean to be rude."

"That's okay." Britt offered a smile that did nothing to hide the anger in her eyes and warned that the interaction between them was far from okay. "I'd be equally as unpleasant, if I'd just figured out what Marco was pulling on the job front. I wondered how long it would take you."

Caitlyn released her breath in a sigh. She shouldn't ask. Shouldn't play into Britt's game. "Found out what?" she asked wearily.

The other woman took her time, savoring each word. "That this project they've dumped in your lap is a put-on. I mean, doesn't it just bug you right down to the bones that you're stuck working in that dump of a warehouse all because Marco wants to keep you away from Lazz?" She smiled knowingly. "Not that it's worked, because here you are."

It took every ounce of self-control not to react, not to hit out and cause any further talk that might find its way into *The Snitch*. "Excuse me, won't you?" she said, and swept past Britt's desk and into Lazz's office.

Caitlyn closed the door behind her and leaned against it, struggling to calm down. So much for friendship. Francesca had warned her, but she'd hoped against hope to prove her sister-in-law wrong. That Britt would work through whatever lingering issues stood between them. But maybe there was no working through them. Caitlyn found it a hard fact to accept.

"Caitlyn?" Lazz shot to his feet. "What's happened? You look like hell."

She almost confided in Lazz and explained the issues between her and Britt. But she hesitated to involve him. She and Britt might not be friends any longer, but she didn't want to cost the other woman her job. Suddenly aware of the file she clutched, she used that as an excuse to explain her distress.

"There are some documents you need to see." She crossed the room and offered him the file. "I came across this when I was going through a bunch of family records stored at the warehouse."

Lazz took the folder and flipped it open. Waving her toward the chair across from his desk, he took a seat and began reading. "Holy hell," he muttered. "What was the old man thinking?"

"Did you know about this contract?"

"Not even a little."

Interesting. "Do you think Primo knew?" she asked.

"Are you kidding? He'd have killed my father if he'd found out."

He glanced at her with eyes the exact same shade of hazel as Marco's. And yet they were nothing like her husband's. Where Marco's held all the warmth and passion of a Mediterranean summer, his twin brother's struck her as cool and remote as a mountain lake. The realization left her momentarily stunned. Why had she never noticed the difference before?

"Have you told anyone?" he asked.

She struggled to focus her attention on Lazz and answer his question. "About the document? No, not a soul. I brought it straight to you."

"What about Marco?"

"I haven't said a word," she told him, more sharply this time. "And you have no idea how guilty that makes me feel."

"This has nothing to do with him and I want it to stay that way." His voice reflected the same sharpness as hers. "I'd like your promise on that. I need time to decide how to handle the situation."

"You have it."

"I'd also like you to hold on to this contract while I consider my options. I'd rather not keep this file in my office where someone might stumble across it."

"No problem. I'll put it back in the box where I found it."

After handing her the folder, he didn't speak but studied her in silence while he made up his mind about something. The moment stretched long enough to put her on edge. She saw the instant he'd reached his decision.

"I felt something that morning, you know," he surprised her by saying.

She shook her head in genuine bewilderment. "I have no idea what you're talking about."

"In the conference room. The morning after you married Marco." He came out from behind his desk to join her and edged his hip on the corner nearest her chair. "I don't believe in The Inferno. At least, I never have. But that morning..."

She could guess where he was going with this and dismissed it with a shake of her head. "The only thing you felt that morning was anger and perhaps a touch of jealousy."

"True. But I also felt a tingle." He rubbed his thumb across his palm and frowned. "Right here."

"I don't know who's set off your little Inferno detector," she replied, gesturing toward his palm. "But it wasn't me. It's not possible." Or was it that she didn't want it to be possible? Because if Lazz felt it, too, it would be proof that The Inferno didn't work.

His brow creased in genuine bewilderment. "Well, there wasn't anyone else there who could have set it off."

"You Dantes and your itchy palms. Do you feel it now?" She put more than a hint of exasperation into the question.

"Maybe." His brows drew together. "A little."

"Well, Marco doesn't feel it a little. If he's not careful, he's going to rub himself raw."

Lazz's mouth tilted upward at the corner. "You sound like a mother hen." Then his amusement faded, replaced by an emotion she didn't want to see in any man's eyes but one. And it wasn't the man lounging in front of her. "I was going to propose that night, you know."

"I know," she whispered.

"It should have been us in front of a priest."

"No, it shouldn't have."

She'd never been more certain of anything in her life. The insight came in a bittersweet rush, and she shut her eyes, accepting what she'd been steadfastly denying for weeks now. It didn't matter whether or not The Inferno was real, or whether or not she believed in it. It didn't matter that she hadn't followed Gran's directives before marrying. Or that she'd chosen a charmer instead of someone more logical and down-to-earth like Lazz. None of it mattered, but one simple fact. Her breath caught, stumbled.

She loved Marco.

"Caitlyn?"

"Oh, God." Tears filled her eyes and leaked into her voice as she shot to her feet. "I am such a fool."

He straightened. "It's okay. Don't cry." He wrapped his arms around her shoulders and patted awkwardly. "We can fix this. I'll find you a lawyer. It'll all work out."

"No. You don't understand." She lifted her head and looked at him. Truly looked at him. How could she have ever thought she couldn't tell one brother from the other? They were nothing alike. Felt nothing the same. "I love him, Lazz."

"Aw, hell. That's not good."

"No. What's not good is you having your hands on my wife." The door banged closed behind Marco. "I suggest you remove them before I remove them for you."

Nine

Marco fought against a blinding rage. Fought to keep his hands off his brother so he didn't do something one of them would barely live to regret. Caitlyn was his wife. *His*. Lazz had no business touching her, and he'd explain that fact in language his brother couldn't mistake.

"You're being ridiculous," Caitlyn said.

He spared her a brief glance. "Don't. Don't act like I'm the one at fault when I walk in and discover you in my brother's arms." He transferred his attention to his twin. "For some truly annoying reason, you're still touching my wife."

Swearing, Lazz held up his hands and took a step back. "Satisfied now?"

"I won't be satisfied until I've pounded less identical into your face."

"So Caitlyn can tell the difference between us?" Lazz bit off a laugh. "Trust me. She's not the least confused on that front."

Marco formed his hands into fists. "I think I'll just make sure of that fact."

Caitlyn stepped between the two brothers, the one place she least belonged. "Could we please bring the testosterone level down a notch? Lazz, you're not helping a bit. Marco, there's a very simple explanation for all this."

"Which is?"

"Well…"

She lifted an eyebrow at Lazz, who shook his head. A flash of annoyance flitted across her face, though it was nothing compared to Marco's annoyance that she needed his brother's approval before explaining the situation.

"I can't tell you," Caitlyn said, a statement that succeeded in shooting Marco's temper straight through the roof. "But I assure you, it's strictly business."

"Lazz with his arms around you was strictly business?" He struggled to rein in his fury. "'Strictly business' made you cry?"

"That was…" She faltered. "That was something else."

"I think it's time I clarified matters," Marco said. "Just in case there are any lingering questions."

"Marco—"

He cut her off with a sweep of his hand. "No, this needs to be said. The wound can't heal until the poison's been drawn out." He turned on his brother. "In case you missed the announcement, Caitlyn and I are married now, Lazz. We're in the process of building a life together. And I won't let anyone, particularly not my own brother, dismantle so much as a single brick of what Caitlyn and I have struggled to cement in place. You are not to interfere in our marriage again. Am I clear on this point?"

Marco watched the war waging across his brother's face. Even though he understood why Lazz found it so difficult to let go, this needed to end, here and now. In the past his family had always had his back, just as he'd always had theirs. He never had to question their unconditional loyalty and support. He wanted that assurance again, to trust implicitly instead of constantly checking behind him to see whether someone had stuck a knife between his shoulder blades.

He waited for Lazz's response, waited for the poison to well up, a poison that had been left to fester for far too long. Finally, it erupted, spilled over in messy waves.

"You took her from me. You lied to her!" Lazz accused. "You went after her like some thief in the night and tricked her into marrying you. She should have the choice to leave, if she wants."

Marco inclined his head. "I agree. But what you don't understand, what you continue to ignore, is that she has always had the choice to leave. And yet she stays with me. There's a reason for that, Lazz. And that reason is why you need to step aside." He let his comments sink in before adding, "She was never yours. You tried to convince yourself she was, tried to bind her to you. But from the moment you first saw her, it was already too late."

"I planned to marry her!"

Didn't Lazz get it? "Even if she left me now, she

would still never be yours. Not in the way you want, not the way a wife should be. I would always stand between you. And if not me, then the ghost of our relationship."

"Isn't that what I'm doing?" Lazz hit back. "Standing between the two of you? Isn't that why you're so jealous, because I had a relationship with her?"

Marco shook his head. "You know it wasn't a true relationship. Caitlyn and I settled that issue long ago. You're not part of our marriage, Lazz. What you had with her was merely an illusion."

Stubbornness clung to Lazz's face. "Only because you interfered."

Marco tried again to get through to his brother. "If you'd taken the relationship further than those first few steps, it would have eventually fallen apart. The woman you are meant to have hasn't come into your life yet. But, I swear to you, Lazz. You will know her when she does. And when that happens you'll realize that what you feel for Caitlyn is a pale imitation of the real thing."

"That's enough, Marco. You've made your point." Once again Caitlyn placed herself between the two men. "Lazz, I realize this is your office, but could you give Marco and me a minute, please?"

He hesitated just long enough to nudge Marco's temper back into the hot zone, before nodding. "Sure."

The minute they were alone, Caitlyn caught Marco's hand in hers. "Listen to me. I promise you, the information I relayed to Lazz was confidential and absolutely business related. If you want to know more, you'll have to discuss it with him, since it's his information to share."

"Why were you crying?" He could still see lingering

traces of her tears. That troubled him more than anything, and he could only think of one explanation. He steeled himself against that possibility. "Was it because of us? Because of our marriage?"

"I was…I was happy crying."

She was holding something back. He could tell. Just as he could tell that her tears weren't ones of pure joy. "Then answer me this, *cara*. Why were you happy crying with your brother-in-law instead of with your husband?"

"It just sort of hit me while I was in here." This time when she looked at him he couldn't mistake the unwavering certainty in her gaze. "I don't regret our marriage. I don't wish I'd married Lazz instead of you, in case there's still any question. But there is an issue we need to clarify."

"Which is?"

"It's this project I've been assigned, and how it came about."

She caught him off guard with the change in subject. He could guess the direction she was headed with this, and it wasn't a place he cared to go. "And?"

She hesitated, no doubt organizing her thoughts. He'd always found it one of her more endearing characteristics. Until now. "You should know that my career gives me security and independence, and I have a serious problem being kept in the dark about decisions that affect my job."

"I thought you were happy with your new assignment," he offered cautiously.

A hint of fire sparked in her blue eyes. "You're missing the point—deliberately, I think. I love my job, both old and new. But I've worked hard to get where I am and I refuse to be sidetracked. My career ensures that I don't have to depend on anyone for anything. I'll always know that if something should happen at some point down the road, like it did with Gran, I can take care of myself."

His mouth tightened. "In other words, if some charmer—me, for instance—sweeps in and tries to sell you a ticket for the next ride over the rainbow, you'll have a pot of gold stashed away to fall back on." He cocked his head to one side. "Close?"

"Dead on."

"Just where the hell did you get the idea I'm trying to interfere with your job security?"

She released his hand and turned toward Lazz's desk. A folder rested on the edge, and she played with the cover. "Tell me something, Marco. Who arranged for me to head this new project, a project supposedly no one else on the face of the planet is capable of successfully completing but me?" She shoved the folder to one side and shot him a keen look. "It was you, wasn't it? You asked my supervisor to use me on this job."

Over the past several days he'd begun to pick up on his wife's moods. Her eyes gleamed the most brilliant shade of teal whenever something satisfied her. And they darkened to indigo whenever heartache threatened. Worry caused her to nibble at her lower lip—something he was quick to put a stop to. He had personal designs on that lip, as he took pains to show her on a regular basis. But most telling of all were the danger signals that flashed, warning of her anger. And holy hell, they might as well be flashing bright red right now.

"Yes, I asked that you be assigned this new project," he informed her.

"In order to keep me away from Lazz?"

"Huh." He pretended to give it some thought. "If that was my goal, it doesn't seem to be working, does it? Because here you are."

His flippancy didn't go over well. "This is serious, Marco. The morning after we were married you told me you wanted me to keep my distance from Lazz and that you'd make certain it happened. Is this your way of making certain? So much for trust."

He answered truthfully. "It's not you I don't trust. It's my brother. In case you didn't notice, he's feeling a bit raw right now. I don't want you in the middle, despite how often you feel the need to put yourself there. This project should only take you a month or two to organize, and to be honest, I can't think of anyone more qualified to head it up. By the time you have it under control— and it is a critical project, by the way, not crayons and busy work—the family dynamics will have settled down and returned to normal. Especially after our little talk here today. At that point, you're free to resume your old job."

"Funny. I don't remember being in on that discussion when it happened."

"Yeah." He thrust a hand through his hair. "It's possible you didn't get the memo. I'm sorry, *cara*. I should have told you."

"Discussed it with me," she corrected sharply. "Allowed me to have a say in the final decision."

"It wouldn't have changed anything," he informed

her gently. "You would have argued. I would have argued. But in the end I would have won."

She stiffened. "Is that how all the decisions will be made in our marriage?"

"I'm just trying to protect you."

"That didn't answer my question, and I don't need your protection," she protested.

"Yes, you do. You married a Dante, Caitlyn. You may not have realized which one at the time you said 'I do,' but you were well aware when you took your vows that your life would change because of my family. The stories in *The Snitch*, alone, should have warned you of that."

Temper flashed to the boiling point. "And part of marrying a Dante is having my decisions made for me? Thanks, but no thanks."

"Enough, Caitlyn. I promised to consult you in the future. And I will. Just as you're going to promise me that you won't use my brother's shoulder for anymore happy tears."

"No one's shoulder but yours?"

"I'll try and bear up under the strain." He hesitated. Since they were clearing the air, this struck him as a good time to warn her about his own job change. "There's some other news I should tell you about."

"Tell me...or warn me?"

"A little of both, I suppose. I consider it good news, though knowing *The Snitch*, they'll find a way to put a negative spin on it." He watched her closely, hoping to gauge her reaction to the news. "I've decided to turn my international duties over to Lazz. Since he's already put in extensive time dealing with our foreign offices, it made the most sense."

A hint of worry edged into her eyes. "But, why? I thought you loved your job."

"I do. Unfortunately, it means I'm out of the country more often than I'm home. I didn't mind before we met, but I don't like being away from you so often or for so long. It's not healthy for a marriage."

Caitlyn removed the folder from Lazz's desk and tucked it under her arm. "Does this have anything to do with keeping Lazz and me apart?"

"Let's consider that an added bonus."

She closed her eyes for a brief instant. "Oh, Marco." She looked at him then, gazing with such sorrow that he flinched. "After everything that's been said here today, this still isn't over, is it?"

"You and Lazz? Over and done. Some of our issues?" He couldn't lie. "Let's just say we have a ways to go yet."

Over the next several days it became clear to Caitlyn that a rift had formed between her and Marco, one they found difficult to bridge. When they came together each night, she sensed a desperation behind their lovemaking as each of them struggled to find a way to repair the damaged connection. To make matters worse, Marco announced that he and Lazz would be flying to Europe for a few days to help smooth over the transition of duties.

"I'll be back next Friday night." Experience had him making short work of packing his bags. "When I return we settle this once and for all."

Before he left, he took her in his arms and kissed her in a way that knocked down barriers and left her hoping that maybe, just maybe, their marriage would work out. And then he was gone.

The week passed at a crawl, and Caitlyn used the opportunity to make significant strides with the warehouse project. She set aside the personal files she'd unearthed, including the contract she'd shown Lazz, and focused instead on reorganizing her team. By midweek, she'd gotten the transfer from paper to digital moving along at a record pace. In a few days she would have the time and focus necessary to go through the box of personal files more carefully in order to decide what to do with the contents.

Friday morning she headed into work feeling more cheerful than she had in days. Marco was due home that evening and she couldn't wait. The time had come to face facts. She loved Marco, loved him with all her heart. It didn't matter anymore how their marriage had come about. What mattered was where they took it from here.

Entering her office, she picked up the box of files she'd sidelined over the past week and set it on her desk. And that's when she saw it. Someone had gotten to her office ahead of her and left an early edition of *The Snitch* on her desk. She almost trashed it, unread. But the headlines caught her eye and she sat down to read. Twenty minutes later she jumped up and went flying out the door. With Marco in Europe, she had his car at her disposal and she headed straight over to the main office building. Once there, she hastened to Britt's desk, a desk occupied by Angie.

"Where's Britt?" Caitlyn demanded.

Angie stared at her in confusion. "I thought she was with you. She asked if I'd cover her desk while she went over to the warehouse."

Caitlyn inhaled sharply. The warehouse. The warehouse where sitting on her desk were files that were a literal goldmine of information for *The Snitch*'s snitch. She fought to stay calm and think. First off, she needed help. Marco and Lazz were out of the country. Sev was in New York with Francesca. That left Nicolò.

A single phone call confirmed that he hadn't arrived at work yet, which left her on her own. She thought fast and then headed for the legal department, hoping against hope that Marco had gotten them working on that confidentiality agreement. She could have kissed the man when he handed it over without a qualm. Next she requested that a notary be located and sent to the warehouse. And then she made a beeline for the exit, struggling not to panic as she went tearing back to her office.

She already knew what she'd find, despite praying she'd be proven wrong. Sure enough, Britt sat in Caitlyn's chair, her feet resting on the desktop, one of the personal files Caitlyn had protected with such care open in her lap.

"Put it down," she snapped out the order.

Britt simply grinned. "Wow. You look a bit peeved. Bad morning?"

"I'm not going to ask you again, Britt."

"Funny. I don't remember you asking me the first time." She dropped her feet to the floor but didn't close the file. "This makes for fascinating reading."

Caitlyn retrieved the document she'd picked up from legal and slapped it in front of Britt. "I've called for a notary. She'll be here in the next few minutes. When she arrives, you're going to sign this."

"Let me guess. It's a confidentiality agreement." Britt shook her head. "Too little, too late, I'm afraid."

"We'll see."

"You know…something's been bugging me."

Caitlyn lifted an eyebrow. "Bugging you down to the bones? Isn't that one of the lines you used in your latest article for *The Snitch*? As soon as I read it, I knew it had to be you. You used that expression when we last spoke."

"Caught that, did you?" Britt lifted a shoulder. "I wondered when I wrote it if you would."

"What did you do? Listen at the door when Lazz, Marco and I had our disagreement? There are too many accurate quotes in that article for it to have happened any other way."

"You all made it so easy for me. Why shouldn't I take advantage of the opportunity?" She waved that aside. "You know, I've been curious for some time why everyone's in such an uproar over my stories. I mean who cares what *The Snitch* prints about the Dantes? It's free publicity. It sure as hell hasn't hurt sales from what I've seen and heard."

"It's affecting Dantes' expansion into the European market."

"Yes, Lazz was kind enough to explain that part to me. But what I didn't get for the longest time is why the Romanos care about what *The Snitch* prints. What's it to them, anyway?"

"They're protecting their reputation."

Britt snapped her fingers. "Truer words have never been spoken. And would you like to know precisely what they're protecting?" She leaned across the desk and whispered, "The Romanos are broke."

"You're making that up."

Britt shook her head. "No, I'm not. Ironic, isn't it?" She leaned back in Caitlyn's chair and folded her arms behind her head. "Marco's spent all this time and money to win their patronage and the Romanos can't even afford a nickel-plated nose ring, let alone a Dantes original."

"How in the world could you possibly know anything about the state of the Romanos' finances, Britt? You write for a penny-ante scandal sheet."

"Oh, I have a few European contacts. According to them, rumors about Vittorio Romano have been floating around for quite a while now. But the Romanos still have an amazing amount of influence over there." Her hand fluttered through the air. "Italian royalty and all that. They've managed to squelch any negative talk. But that won't last much longer." She tapped the file she held. "Unless, of course, they decide to force Lazz to honor his father's little business contract. Won't *The Snitch* readers find that a fascinating little tidbit."

An idea came to Caitlyn, as though a gift from on high. Not just how to stop Britt, but how to use her as she'd been using Dantes. She just needed a few minutes to think. To organize the various pieces into a logical whole.

"I don't think your readers will find your next story interesting at all," Caitlyn said with exquisite calm.

"Because you're not going to print it. In fact, your days writing about the Dantes are about to end."

Britt's eyebrows shot upward. "And you're going to somehow end them?"

"Well… The way I figure it, the Romanos—those same Romanos who have such an amazing amount of influence—will have a bit more sway over here than you might think. And I'm guessing they're not going to be too happy when I tell them what you're about to do. I'm also willing to bet that you're going to find yourself in an even more uncomfortable position now that you're outed as *The Snitch*'s snitch. What use will you be to the tabloid when Dantes fires you? Or sues you for defamation? The Romanos might not have the money to pursue legal action, but I assure you that the Dantes can afford it, and then some."

Britt gave a careless shrug, but a hint of worry flickered behind her eyes. "I still have plenty of ammunition to sell to *The Snitch*."

"It's going to run out eventually," Caitlin pointed out. "And then where will you be? I doubt *The Snitch* is going to keep you around when you can't deliver the goods any longer."

Britt's expression turned shrewd. "I gather this is leading somewhere? Maybe a deal of some sort?"

Caitlyn nodded. "You leave the Romanos alone, as well as forget all about that contract you found, and I'll give you a huge final story. A really special one."

"I don't know…" Britt caressed the folder she held. "The story I just found is pretty darn special. Why would I give it up?"

"That contract is twenty years old. It isn't worth the paper it's written on. Plus, although the Romanos might get big play in Europe, the average American reader doesn't know them. Why would *Snitch* readers care whether some aristocratic European family is struggling financially? Your editor isn't going to pay much for that story. Trust me, Britt. The one I have in mind is far better."

Avarice gleamed in Britt's eyes. "How much better?"

"A dream come true."

Suspicion tempered her greed. "If your story is so much better, why are you willing to trade it for the Romanos? I must be missing something."

"For one reason and one reason only. It will salvage Marco's deal, and I'll do anything to help my husband."

She didn't say anything more, but waited to see if the other woman would take the bait. For a minute Caitlyn didn't think it would happen. Then greed won out.

"This had better be good, or it's all going in."

Caitlyn shook her head. "You're going to sign that confidentiality agreement. After this story, you're done writing about the Dantes and their associates." She almost laughed at the sly expression in Britt's eyes. "Don't bother looking for a loophole. Marco had Legal create a nice, airtight document. Knowing them, you probably can't even speak the Dante name without serious repercussions."

Britt moistened her lips. "Is your story that good?" At Caitlyn's nod, she pressed. "First, I need a hint."

"Fair enough. Ever heard of Dantes' Inferno?"

Britt's eyes widened. "Once. When I asked Lazz about it, he clammed up and I couldn't pry another word out of him."

Caitlyn raised an eyebrow. "I take it we have a deal?"

"Absolutely."

"Just one other question while we wait for the notary."

Britt grimaced. "I can guess. You want to know why. Why would I betray the darling Dantes after all they've done for me." She rolled her eyes. "Would you like me to make up some sob story about a poor, sick mother? How about a desperately ill child? Would that satisfy you?"

"The truth will do."

"Oh, come on, Caitlyn. Why do you think?" She caressed the earrings she wore, earrings she'd bragged about during lunch that fateful day Marco had swept her off to Nevada. The fire diamonds licked coldly across Britt's earlobes. "I got ticked off when Marco and Lazz wouldn't give me the time of day but were all over you. Seemed to me selling my stories to *The Snitch* was the only way I was going to get my hands on the Dante jewels, even if they weren't the ones I'd originally had in mind." Then she had the nerve to wink.

The notary arrived a short time later and Britt signed the confidentiality agreement. The minute they were alone again, she leaned forward. "Just so you know, I'm going to quote you, word for word. Your name's going to be all over this article so that everyone knows it was you who betrayed Marco and the Dante family. You may be Mrs. High-and-Mighty Dante now. But how long do you think your marriage will last once your husband finds out what you've done?"

Caitlyn didn't have any doubt about that. It would last about as long as Britt's future at Dantes.

Ten

Caitlyn had planned to tell Marco what happened with Britt the instant he walked through the door. To explain what she'd done and why. But the longer it took for him to return home, the less she wanted to confess her sins. Pacing through the empty apartment, she faced some hard, cold facts.

Her actions today, even though she'd tried to base them on the better good of Dantes, would damage her relationship with Marco, perhaps irreparably. She could explain that she'd attempted to choose the lesser of two evils, but in all honesty she'd made some huge mistakes along the way. For one thing she'd confronted Britt on her own without consulting the Dantes first. Granted, there hadn't been anyone *to* consult when she'd reached her decision. But that didn't change the fact that it wasn't her decision to make.

Worse, she'd told Britt about The Inferno. Would Marco understand that she'd revealed the information with the best of intentions? Would he understand that she'd thought it would protect the Romanos, in addition to the Dantes European expansion? That she had a plan in mind when she'd made the revelation?

Or would he believe she'd put a friend before family loyalty? That her doubts about The Inferno had led her to be indiscreet? Because if there was one thing that she and Marco agreed to disagree about, it was The Inferno.

Still, that didn't mean she had to tell him what she'd done the minute he walked in the door, she suddenly realized. This night could still be theirs. All she had to do was remain silent until morning.

His key sounded in the lock and the next instant he was there, filling the apartment with body and spirit. Filling her heart to overflowing. "Why are you standing here in the dark?" He dropped his bags just inside the door and kicked it closed behind him. "*Cara?* Is something wrong?"

"No." She couldn't do it. She couldn't hide what she'd done from him. "Yes."

He was by her side before the words had even left her lips. His arms closed around her and she simply melted. Everything about him ripped her to pieces, shredded her emotions and then put them back together again. With one touch he turned her world upside down and sent everything safe and rational spinning into chaos. And with the next touch he made that world right again, made her realize that this was where she belonged. In his arms, tucked close to his heart.

She inhaled the crisp, delicious scent of him, filling her lungs until she was dizzy with it. She'd missed him, been empty without him. And more than anything, she needed his hands on her. Needed to feel him moving over her, the sweet dichotomy of male in life-affirming opposition to female. To hear desperate Italian endearments ripping through that deep, lyrical voice. To watch those beautiful angled features harden with passion, while the burn of want swept into his eyes and set them afire with sparks of gold and amber and jade.

She forced herself to ignore the yearning and tell him what she'd done. "Something happened today that I need to discuss with you."

"Stop." He covered her mouth with his fingers. "I've been gone a week. First things first."

He cupped her face and lifted her for his kiss. With a soft moan she opened to him, welcoming him home. He swept inward with lazy intent, nipping playfully, and she tumbled headlong into the embrace. Thrusting her fingers deep into his thick hair, she angled her head for better access and whispered her encouragement. His playfulness faded, replaced with blatant hunger.

At least here, when they came together like this, they were perfectly attuned. She only wished it could be enough. With a sigh of regret, she turned her head aside. "We need to talk first. We can have sex afterward." Assuming he still wanted to.

"No."

Surprise had her looking at him. "No?"

"No, damn it." Frustration ate through his words. "It's not just sex and you know it. From the moment we first touched it's always been something more than that."

"The Inferno."

"Is that so hard to accept?"

"Funny you should mention that. I—"

He took her hand in his and locked it, palm to palm, with his. "Tell me you don't feel that."

She closed her eyes, shivering. Heat warmed the center of her hand, sinking deep inward and sending desire screaming through her body. "It's you. Just you."

"Someday you'll admit the truth." He stopped her before she could argue. "I know, I know. Fairy tales aren't truth."

"Marco—"

"Later. Right now I'm going to give you a taste of happily-ever-after. And if that's not enough to convince you, we'll start over again with once-upon-a-time. And I will tell you the tale again and again until you're convinced it's real, no matter how long it takes."

With that he swept her up and carried her through to the bedroom. They tumbled to the mattress together, locked in each other's arms. He found her mouth again and worried at her bottom lip before seducing her with slow, drugging kisses.

She fumbled with the knot of his tie and loosened it, stripping away the length of silk before tackling the buttons of his shirt. He moved to help and she chased his hands away, rolling until she was on top. "No. It's my turn. Let me do this for you."

One by one, she slipped button through hole, pushing

aside the soft cotton. Heaven help her, but he was a beautiful man. She never tired of looking at him, of touching the delicious male contours that were so different from her own. She traced a path over his smooth chest, easing the shirt from his shoulders. He lifted onto his elbows so she could sweep it aside.

He remained silently watchful, his expression giving nothing away. Not that he'd remain impassive for long. She'd see to that. She lowered her head to trail kisses down the center of his chest. Then lower still. Without a word she unbelted his trousers and stripped him. And then she gave him the most intimate kiss of all.

She heard the harsh groan, the choked sound he made when he attempted to push out her name. His fingers forked into her hair. She resisted their tug, intent on giving him as much pleasure as he had given her over the past weeks. His voice filled the air, the Italian poetic in its expressiveness, ripe with power. She didn't have to understand the words to hear the desperate plea behind them. And then the tenor changed, became demand, a demand she found impossible to resist.

He dragged her upward, making short work of the few garments she wore. She expected him to take her then, fast and frantic. He must have read her thoughts because he simply shook his head.

"I can't," he told her. "This is too important to rush. Don't you understand? I want these times we spend together to last, so I can relish every moment of them. They're beautiful and intimate. These are the times I feel closest to you. Why would I rush that? That's not how I want you. It never has been."

He watched as confusion came, then eased. "We're dancing again, aren't we?" she asked in sudden understanding. "The goal isn't getting to point Z."

He caught the reference from one of their discussions early in their marriage and smiled in response. "No, it's not. It's all the points in between that are most important."

Mischief sparkled within her eyes. "Are you sure about that?"

He nuzzled the soft curve of her breast. "Point Z is inevitable in all things, not just making love. But to fully enjoy the culmination you have to savor each step in between. And that's what I plan for tonight. To savor you, *cara*."

"Oh, Marco."

Tears sparkled in her eyes and he saw something there he'd waited a long time to see. Did she even realize she loved him? Or did fear keep her from acknowledging it the way it kept her from acknowledging the truth of The Inferno?

If she couldn't see it for herself, he'd have to show her in every possible way. Time slipped softly by, an unnoticed tempo to the points along the way as Marco lingered over each step of their lovemaking. He adored kissing her silken skin, worshiping it with lips, tongue and teeth. Loved the contrast of fine-boned strength that lay just beneath the lush roundness of feminine curves.

She called so sweetly to him as her climax approached, and that night the song she sang as she went over was unlike anything he'd ever heard before. He wanted to spend a lifetime drawing that song from her.

Moving to it. Making love to it. Creating endless harmonies to accompany it.

Night filled the room when they exchanged a long, leisurely kiss and drifted into an exhausted slumber, arms and legs entwined. Marco smoothed his hand down his wife's spine and tucked her close. She wiggled against him, pillowing her head in the crook of his arm.

She murmured something in her sleep, something remarkably like, "I love you, Marco."

"I love you, too, *cara*," he whispered. And then he slept.

Marco woke not long after dawn, the soft burr of his cell phone pulling him from a deep, peaceful sleep. Swearing beneath his breath, he carefully eased himself from his wife's embrace and snatched up the phone. Then he padded naked into the living room.

"This better be important," he growled.

"Where's Caitlyn?" Nicolò asked in abrupt Italian.

Marco glanced over his shoulder. The bedroom remained shrouded in silence. "The same place I should be." He answered in Italian, as well. "In our bed. Asleep."

"Listen, you need to come down to Dantes. We've got a problem."

"What's it got to do with Caitlyn?"

"How do you know—"

"You asked where she was. You'd only have done that if whatever's going on somehow involves her." At his brother's continued silence, Marco snapped, "Does it?"

"We'll explain when you get here."

Jet lag ate at the frayed edges of his temper. "You'll explain now."

"I can't do that. Won't," he corrected. "There's something you need to see. To read."

"And whatever this something is has to do with Caitlyn?"

"Yes." Nicolò paused. "And Marco? We'd appreciate it if you didn't mention this meeting to your wife."

Marco didn't know what the hell was going on, but he suspected he wasn't going to like whatever his brothers had to say to him. In fact, he knew he wouldn't. After quietly dressing he scribbled a quick note to Caitlyn, in case she woke before he returned, informing her he'd be back in an hour or so. Then he drove to Dantes.

His three brothers were all waiting for him when he arrived, grouped around the smoked-glass conference table off Lazz's office. He examined them one by one. Sev appeared troubled, and sat silent and tense. Lazz looked equally concerned, and that worried Marco since he suspected that his twin still had feelings for Caitlyn, even if they now leaned toward a more brotherly regard. If Lazz had aligned himself with Sev and Nicolò, that didn't bode well for Caitlyn. Worst of all, Nicolò, the family trouble-shooter, quietly steamed, his eyes black with anger.

Nicolò took the lead, spinning a well-thumbed copy of *The Snitch* across the length of the table toward Marco. "That edition came out yesterday, before you and Lazz returned home. Read it."

Taking his time, Marco gave the article his full attention. Fury boiled through him with each successive word. "What the hell is this?" he demanded. "How could they know what happened that day in Lazz's office? There were only three—"

"Exactly," Nicolò pronounced.

Marco's head jerked up. "You can't think…" They did think. Every last one of them. "No way. No damn way did Caitlyn hand this information over to *The Snitch*. She wouldn't do it."

Next Nicolò shot several typed pages stapled together in a thin packet down the table toward Marco. "Now read this. I don't think you were meant to find it until Monday. But I came into work today to leave some papers in your office and found it sitting on your desk."

Reluctantly Marco picked up the papers. *Dantes' Inferno,* screamed the title. *Marco's bride tells all.* He read every last word. The innuendos. The endless quotes. The underlying mockery that clung like slime to every sentence. Through it all he looked for key phrases. Phrases like "fantasy" or "superstition" or "fairy tale." But they weren't there. He sucked in a slow, calming breath before lifting his gaze to his brothers'.

"So?" he said with a shrug. "She didn't do this, if that's what you're asking."

Nicolò shoved back his chair. "How can you say that?" he challenged in disgust. "Because she's your Inferno bride? Because once she's been struck by the family curse, she wouldn't dream of betraying us?"

"Blessing," Marco and Sev said in unison.

Nicolò swore. "This is serious. There were only three of you in Lazz's office the day you had that argument. Lazz says that most of what *The Snitch* has quoted is accurate."

"It is," Marco reluctantly confirmed.

"Now we have advance copy on the next article and once again Caitlyn is quoted."

"That doesn't mean—"

"I called the paper, Marco! I asked them about it and they've admitted this is the exact same article their reporter turned in to them, although they refused to identify her. *Her*," he repeated. "They're planning to run this story in their next edition. Now, are you still going to tell me Caitlyn's innocent in all this?"

"Ah, guys—" Lazz began.

Marco waved him silent and shot to his feet. "You want me to explain how I know she isn't involved?"

"Oh, please." Nicolò folded his arms across his chest. "This I've got to hear."

"Fine. I'll tell you." Marco planted his hands on the table and leaned in, speaking with absolute conviction. "I know Caitlyn didn't do this because I know my wife. Not because of The Inferno. But because I've lived with her. Worked with her. Spent time with her. And she's as honest and decent and honorable as the day is long. Nothing you can say will convince me that she betrayed us."

"Marco—"

"Stay out of this Lazz." He locked gazes with Nicolò. "Now are we through here?"

Nicolò's smile was harder than Marco had ever seen it before. "I'm not sure. Why don't we ask your wife."

Marco froze. Caitlyn was here? Why hadn't he felt her? Why hadn't he sensed her presence? The Inferno had always worked as a warning system before this. He spun around and found her standing there. Just standing there, looking more devastated than he'd thought possible.

He shook his head in confusion. "*Cara?* What are you doing here?"

"Marco," she whispered.

And then he knew.

He'd believed her.

It was everything Caitlyn could do to keep from crying. During all the weeks of their marriage, she'd longed for proof that what he felt for her emanated from more than The Inferno. And now, at long last, he'd done just that. How bitterly ironic that he'd been wrong.

"I can explain," she said. "Britt Jones is the snitch."

"And you told Britt about The Inferno."

"Yes. She'd gotten into some files I had. Personal documents of your father's." She spared Lazz a swift glance and saw horrified comprehension dawn on his face. "I…I traded her the information."

"You gave her The Inferno?" Nicolò interrupted, furiously. "Why the hell would you do that? What could possibly have been in those files that made it more advantageous to tell her about private Dante business?"

"It was some rather damning information about the Romanos and your father." Lazz began to explain, but Caitlyn overrode him. The details of the contract weren't what mattered. She needed Marco to understand the impossible situation she'd been in, and how and why she'd made her decision. "When I read the latest copy of *The Snitch,* I realized Britt was responsible for the leaks. It couldn't have been anyone else. I swear I didn't know it was her before then. When I confronted her, she admitted it."

"Why the hell didn't you tell one of us?" Marco asked.

"I tried. None of you were there. Not even Nicolò. Britt had information about the Romanos. About the current state of their finances. Marco..." She caught her lower lip between her teeth. "Marco, they're broke."

"We already knew that," he replied. She'd never heard him speak in such a stony, remote fashion. "What we're after is their goodwill. We want their endorsement, their contacts. Their lineage."

Sev held up his hands. "Marco, you have to fly out and talk to Vittorio. Now. Fill him in about The Inferno before he reads about it."

"I'll leave immediately."

"Marco—"

He simply shook his head. Without a word, he left the conference room. Caitlyn followed him, desperate to try again. "Marco, please. Tell Mr. Romano that this will be the final story. I got Britt to sign a confidentiality agreement."

He turned to confront her. "Why didn't you tell me about all this before? Last night, for instance?"

"I was going to tell you." She spared a swift glance over her shoulder to confirm that they were alone. "We...we got distracted."

"I don't have time for this. We'll settle it when I return."

She couldn't let him walk away. Not now. Not like this. If he did, she might never have another chance to fix things. Because if he walked away this time, she didn't think the rift between them would ever be bridged. "Listen to me. I have an idea for how we can spin this. How we can use it as a marketing tool."

He stiffened, his eyes darkening to hard amber

nuggets. "The Inferno isn't something you spin, Caitlyn. It isn't some marketing ploy to sell Dantes jewelry. I'd have thought by now you'd realize that."

For the first time she sensed how flat-out furious he was. "I...I know that."

He stalked closer, practically scorching the air with his wrath. "No, clearly you don't. And that's the whole problem. You seem to think this is an amusing little story we recount over cocktails. It isn't. The Inferno goes to the very heart of who and what we are. It's part of our heritage."

He wrapped his fingers around her wrist and dragged her hand to his chest. Each beat of his heart sank into her palm, the very palm where The Inferno had first blazed. She tried to hold back her tears and failed. "Marco, I'm so sorry. I had to make a fast decision. I realize now it was the wrong one."

He simply shook his head. "Right from the start you've treated The Inferno as though it were a foolish fairy tale. No matter what I've said to you, no matter how many times I've explained it, you refuse to understand its true meaning."

"I understand that it's important to you. I do."

"You still don't get it, Caitlyn." Not *cara,* she noticed. Maybe never again if she couldn't find a way to fix this. "The Inferno is part of me. You can't pluck it free, like a weed that displeases you. When you deny that part of me, you deny me."

"No, I—"

He spoke across her protest. "The time for discussion is over. You have refused to accept The Inferno from the

very start. I thought given time you'd finally understand. That you'd see it was as much a part of you as it
is me." Weariness cut across his expression. "But it
isn't, is it? You don't believe. You indulge me as though
I were a foolish child. Well, no more." He released her,
cutting off her incipient response with a slicing motion
of his hand. *No more.*

She watched as he spun on his heel and walked away.
Watched as he left her without a backward glance. And
all the while she kneaded the palm of her right hand with
the thumb of her left.

Eleven

The next three days were sheer hell for Caitlyn, filled with endless hours in which she combed over every decision, every word of every conversation, as well as those final heartbreaking minutes with Marco. She considered all the alternative choices she could have made and all the possible scenarios that would have resulted from those changes. But no matter which path she chose, she couldn't think of a single one that would have improved the end result.

Except if she'd told Marco she loved him.

She closed her eyes in distress. Maybe that would have made a difference. Maybe that would have made him less furious. Maybe then The Inferno wouldn't have been like an unscalable mountain between them. But she hadn't and he'd left, and she hadn't heard a word from him since. Only time would tell if they'd be able to find a way over that mountain. But with each passing day, the doubts piled up as hope faded.

"Caitlyn?" Nicolò paused in the doorway of her office and leaned a shoulder against the jamb. "Lazz says I need to come and talk to you. That it's urgent."

Caitlyn didn't bother to conceal her relief, though it didn't escape her notice that her brother-in-law didn't actually step foot into her office. "No one's been willing to listen, and there's not a lot of time."

"Yeah, well." He shrugged, gazing at her with eyes so dark a brown they appeared black. She'd never realized before just how disconcerting they were until he trained them on her. "Some of us aren't too happy with your efforts to save us from the Jones woman."

"Really?" Maybe if she hadn't been so tired or worried or downright ticked off, she wouldn't have let her temper get out of control. But it had been a rough few days and the expression on Nicolò's face set her off. Big-time. She stalked across the room toward him. "Isn't it interesting that none of you managed to uncover the mole and deal with her. None of you were forced to come up with a plan to derail Britt on the spur of the moment the way I was. Yet, you're all too happy to point out every last one of my mistakes. After the fact, of course." She planted her hands on her hips. "Well, I don't think I made a mistake. What do you think of that? Now, do you want to come in and find out what I have in mind to salvage this mess? Or are you going to let *The Snitch* win?"

A slight smile eased the sternness of Nicolò's tough-hewn features. "Okay, little sister." He walked into the room and sprawled in the seat in front of her desk. "I'm always interested in hearing creative solutions to impossible problems. Tell me your idea."

Instead of returning to her desk, Caitlyn took the chair next to him and leaned forward. "It's quite simple. The day *The Snitch* is released, the very day, we release a press statement."

"We."

She waved that aside. "Dantes, of course. We agree with everything *The Snitch* says. Yes, there really is an Inferno. Yes, when it strikes, Dantes mate for life. Yes, it's a connection between soul mates."

"I'm curious." He tilted his head to one side and fixed those unnerving eyes on her. "Have you lost your mind?"

Enough was enough. "Just wait for it, Nicolò," she snapped. To her surprise, he did just that. "And then we say that The Inferno's part of what makes Dantes' jewelry so spectacular and so special. We tell all those women out there, all those women who would give their eyeteeth to experience The Inferno, that not only is it real, but everything the Dantes touch is imbued with the passion from The Inferno—from the bracelet and necklace that grace a woman's arms and throat, right down to the fire diamond wedding rings that a man places on his bride's finger."

Nicolò straightened in his chair, his gaze sharpening. "Damn."

"Exactly."

"No, seriously. Damn. That just might work." He thought it through, before nodding. "You came up with all that during your negotiation with the Jones woman? On the fly?" he asked.

"Yes."

"You know what I think?"

"Not a clue."

His smile grew. "I think your talents are totally wasted in the Finance Department."

Marco arrived back in San Francisco so tired he couldn't see straight. In the week he'd been gone, his anger had cooled, if not the pain caused by Caitlyn's decision to tell Britt about The Inferno. He'd endured countless phone calls from each of his brothers, as well as Francesca, Primo and Nonna. Every last one of them had been clear that Britt had acted on her own until that final story, when Caitlyn had taken desperate measures to protect Dantes. And every last one of them supported his wife's decision.

And so did he, he finally admitted to himself. When all was said and done, he loved Caitlyn and he was determined to find a way to make their marriage work. To his relief, Lazz met him outside baggage claim, though his relief turned to annoyance when his brother started in on him about Caitlyn the instant they climbed in the car.

"What you don't seem to understand, Marco, is that she had a plan to turn whatever Britt printed about The Inferno to our advantage." Lazz pulled a face. "Well, that's Caitlyn. She always has a plan."

"And how many times do I have to tell you," Marco responded coldly, "that The Inferno isn't a marketing ploy?"

"You haven't even heard her idea, yet."

Marco scrubbed his hand across his face, striving to push aside his jet lag and focus. "No, you're right. I haven't. So, tell me. What did she come up with?" Lazz gave him the details, and Marco leaned back against his seat, his eyes narrowed against the midday sunshine as he absorbed the details. "That's not half-bad," he conceded at last.

"Not half-bad? Are you kidding me? It'll send women flocking to the stores." Enthusiasm riddled Lazz's voice. "They'll all want their small piece of The Inferno. *The Snitch* is going to be furious at how we've turned this around."

"Even so…" Marco shook his head. "You know how I feel about profiting from The Inferno. And I guarantee Primo feels the same way."

Lazz studied his brother for a long, silent moment. "I've thought about this. Seriously, I have. Caitlyn's idea isn't some loud, brash ploy. It's softer than you're making out. Gentler. It's almost…"

"Almost what?"

"It's almost like she believes in The Inferno."

"We are talking about Caitlyn here, right?"

"That's what makes it so amazing," Lazz said. "This isn't a hard-sell campaign. It's sweet and romantic. And honest."

Marco cocked his head to one side, intrigued. "Honest, how?"

"Well, for one thing, if you truly believe in The Inferno—"

"I do."

"Then, you must believe that our jewelry is imbued with a hint of The Inferno's passion. I mean, think about it, Marco. Didn't Francesca create her most spectacular designs after she fell in love with Sev? Doesn't Primo credit Nonna with the inspiration for his greatest achievements? Don't you think The Inferno influenced them, brought some of that passion to their work?"

Marco couldn't deny it. "You really think that's what inspired her to come up with the marketing campaign?"

Lazz shrugged. "Do you have a better explanation?"

"No."

A sudden idea struck Marco, one so out there that it could only have been a jet-lag-induced flight of whimsy. But the more he considered the possibility, the more viable it became. It offered him the best of all worlds, an avenue for fixing their problem as well as a way to convince his wife that not only did he love her with all his heart and soul, but that she loved him, too. He just needed a few minutes to wrap his poor, tired brain around all the various details and organize them into a semblance of a plan. Unfortunately, details and organization were his wife's specialty, not his.

As soon as he'd thought it through, shuffled some of the pieces around and thought it through some more, he turned to Lazz. "There's something we need to arrange, a small addendum to Caitlyn's idea."

Lazz glanced in his direction. "Aw, hell, Marco. I know that look. Nicolò gets it every time he comes up with one of his crazier schemes. Whatever you're thinking, forget it."

"Not a chance. If it works, it won't only guarantee

Dantes' success, but it may prove to my darling, stubborn, pragmatic wife—hell, to all of you unbelievers—that The Inferno really does exist."

Lazz sighed. "I'm not going to like this idea, am I?"

"Not even a little." But this was important, perhaps the most important scheme he'd ever put together, with one exception—the night he'd convinced Caitlyn to marry him. "The timing on this is vital."

"That's what your wife said."

"No, I mean we need to time our call to Britt Jones very carefully."

"What call to Britt Jones?" Lazz asked in alarm.

"The one where I give her a heads-up about our new marketing plan."

Lazz's jaw dropped. "You're going to *what?*"

"If Britt responds the way I expect her to, not only will our sales double, but more importantly, my wife will realize The Inferno is no fantasy."

Events transpired just as Caitlyn predicted. Britt's final article came out in *The Snitch* to mixed reaction. Some thought it sweet, but most treated The Inferno claims with amused disdain. Dantes' press release broke only hours later and changed all that. To her delight, the story piqued media attention and received impressive coverage under the banner of a light human-interest story.

Women in particular found The Inferno claims quite intriguing, and traffic in and out of the various Dantes stores picked up significantly. Thanks to the extensive media coverage, Marketing and PR arranged for a press conference featuring all of the Dantes, and Caitlyn decided that she had no choice but to join the family on the dais, since she'd been so extensively quoted in Britt's article. No doubt she'd have to field her fair share of questions.

The one thing she hadn't anticipated was seeing Britt among the milling press, a *Snitch* photographer at her side. Her ex-friend made a point of catching Caitlyn's attention in order to offer a cheeky wave, and seemed delighted by the surprise and dismay her appearance engendered.

"Ignore her," Francesca recommended. "She's just living off her five minutes of fame. She doesn't even warrant the usual fifteen."

"After the way she spun The Inferno story, I'd have thought this would be the last place she'd want to show her face." Caitlyn glanced down the row of Dantes. "Lazz looks on the verge of killing her. I think he felt her betrayal as much as I did."

"Probably because she was his personal assistant. That had to hurt."

Caitlyn caught her lip between her teeth. "When does Marco get back from Italy, do you know? I was hoping he'd be here for this."

Francesca gave her an odd look. "Sev said he got back last night. Didn't he—" She broke off at her sister-in-law's expression. "Oh, no. He didn't come home? Caitlyn, I'm so sorry."

As though their conversation summoned him, he appeared on the far end of the dais. He didn't even look her way and Caitlyn's breath hitched in reaction. She blinked hard against a rush of tears. She needed to calm down, to shove her emotions to one side. She didn't dare betray her distress. Not here. Not now. Not in front of all these witnesses.

The next several minutes passed in a haze. She heard various Dantes speak, heard questions being lobbed in, caught and spun back out again. It wasn't until Britt stepped forward that Caitlyn's focus sharpened to pinpoint intensity.

"Hello, Marco," she practically purred. "I just wanted to thank you for your call yesterday."

Caitlyn's head jerked in his direction. "Did you know about that?" she whispered to Francesca.

"No," her sister-in-law murmured in return. "Sev never said a word. And judging by the expression on my dear husband's face, he didn't know, either."

Britt continued to address Marco. "One of the things you said during our conversation was that there wasn't any way to prove or disprove The Inferno. Let's see. How did you phrase it? Something along the lines of 'that was the beauty of your family's scam.'" She laughed. "Oops. I mean, your family legend."

"I believe I said that *you* couldn't disprove it. You really should strive for accuracy when you quote people. I've noticed it's an ongoing problem of yours."

Caitlyn shut her eyes. Oh, Marco. Why did he feel the need to tweak her tail? Hadn't he learned yet how vindictive Britt was?

As though reading Caitlyn's mind, Britt bared her teeth. "Well, surprise, surprise. I have come up with a way to disprove it. Your marketing department claims that a bit of this Inferno is imbued in every piece of jewelry you sell…" She touched her earrings. "Not that you could prove it by me—"

"I suppose there are some people even The Inferno can't help," he offered.

Britt's smile vanished. "Well, I'd like you to prove The Inferno, right here and now."

Marco folded his arms across his chest. "Don't be ridiculous, Britt. How are we supposed to do that?"

"No, no, no," Caitlyn whispered beneath her breath. "He's playing right into her hands."

To her surprise, Francesca began to smile. "Don't be so sure. I have the impression your husband has that woman's number better than you do."

Britt climbed onto the dais, looking thoroughly pleased with herself. "I happen to have the answer to that right here." She opened a voluminous bag she had slung over her shoulder. "I suggest we put it to a little test. You and Lazz are twins. I'd like to see if your wife can pick out which one of you is which, using only The Inferno."

Caitlyn stilled. "I can do that," she told Francesca. "That's simple."

As though Britt had heard, she pulled out a hood and a pair of earplugs. "Without the use of her eyes or ears, of course." Interest rippled through the gathering, and she played to the crowd. "Now, I've tested these myself. She's not going to be able to see or hear anything. Then I want Marco and Lazz to line up in front of her and if she can pick out the right brother, I'll take back every last word I ever said about the Dantes. Even the positive stuff."

"Interesting, but…" He shook his head. "It's not a sweet enough deal. I'm thinking we should go for broke."

"Oh?" Curiosity sparked, along with a hint of amusement. "You want to up the stakes?"

"Absolutely. How about this… You lose, I want every last piece of Dante jewelry you own. I'll even reimburse you for whatever you paid for them." He covered the microphone and his playfulness faded, replaced by a dangerous edge. "You see, Britt, I don't want you wearing anything we've ever crafted. Furthermore, you're banned from ever entering a Dantes store from this day forward."

Humiliation sent hot color streaking across her cheekbones. "And if I win, I want all of you to admit that this whole Inferno business is nothing but a publicity stunt," she announced in ringing tones. "*And* I want you to tear up my confidentiality agreement. I've decided there are a few more articles I'd like to write about you Dantes."

Before Caitlyn had time to beg Marco to turn the offer down, he nodded in agreement. "Done."

Marco turned toward Caitlyn, but Britt stepped between them. "Oh, no, lover boy." An almost vicious note crept into her voice, one that didn't go unnoticed. "I'm not giving you an opportunity to speak to her and arrange for some way of signaling her. We do this my way."

"I have no problem with that," Marco said with an easy shrug.

He glanced over Britt's shoulders toward Caitlyn. She met his look, waiting to see the anger and disillusionment from when they'd parted earlier in the week.

But not a trace of it remained. In its place was something that had tears flooding her eyes again. She saw a calm certainty. There was no doubt in her mind that he believed in her, without hesitation or exception. Before she could do more than stare in bewilderment, Britt crossed to her side.

"I'm going to put Lazz and your husband in front of you. When I tap your shoulder, you point either left or right toward your husband." She leaned in and spoke quietly enough that they couldn't be overheard. "When you lose, my expression of triumph is going to be the first thing you see and my laughter the first thing you hear. And, honey, I flat-out can't wait."

With that, she oversaw the placement of both earplugs and hood, before maneuvering Caitlyn to the center of the dais. There was an endless delay during which she sensed movement around her. And that entire time, she stood frozen in panic.

If Lazz and Marco had been lined up in front of her, even with their backs turned as Francesca had suggested all those weeks ago, Caitlyn no longer questioned her ability to tell one twin from the other. But blindfolded? How was she supposed to pull this off?

And what would happen if she chose wrong? Not much question about that. If she didn't succeed, they'd lose the Romano account for good. The campaign she'd come up with would flop because The Inferno would be disproved. But worst of all, Marco would realize she wasn't really his Inferno bride.

Why had he done this? Why had he looked at her with such confidence, with such...*love*. She stiffened.

Dear God, *that's* what she saw in his eyes when he looked at her. He didn't just believe in her and trust her. He loved her. And because of that love, the crazy man was convinced that she could feel him through the hood, through the earplugs, through everything that separated them. Had he lost his mind?

She could only think of one way—and a darned slim one at that—this might work. Her only hope was to trust in herself and believe that she could sense her husband, as she had the day she'd lunched with Francesca and Nonna. That The Inferno would miraculously help her separate him from Lazz. And with that thought came the realization that she was putting her faith in something she'd always insisted didn't exist.

Somehow, at some point during their marriage, she'd started to believe in the existence of The Inferno. To accept it as fact instead of fiction, truth instead of fairy tale. The breath hitched in her throat. Whatever The Inferno was, she could feel it warming her, connecting her to Marco like a living conduit.

Britt shuffled her into position and tapped her on the shoulder. Caitlyn hadn't a clue why it had taken so long. Not that it mattered. She closed her eyes, despite the blanket of darkness provided by the hood, and focused on Marco. As she did, memories swept through her.

Marco offering his hand in the lobby of Dantes and the two of them experiencing that initial, startling electric shock. Marco on the balcony of Le Premier, kissing her for the very first time while pretending to be Lazz. Their wedding, where he'd gazed down at her with such passion she shivered just recalling it. Their wedding night, a night so beautiful it would be an integral part of her until the day she died. All the intensely passionate nights since, when the two of them had become one. And finally, Marco staring at her before Britt had placed the hood over her head, staring with absolute faith.

With love.

She opened herself to her husband, pausing in confusion when she didn't sense him in either of the two men standing before her. And then she felt the tickle of awareness, not in front, but off to her right. She turned. Hesitated. Felt the distinct throb in her palm. And then she didn't hesitate at all. She made a beeline for her husband.

His arms closed around her, lifted her. And then he stripped off the hood and gently pulled free the earplugs. "Any more questions about whether or not The Inferno exists?" he asked with a broad grin.

"Not a one." Caitlyn wrapped her arms around Marco's neck and kissed him, while cheers erupted all around them. "I love you, Marco."

"I love you, too, *cara,* from the minute we first touched. For the rest of our lives you are my Inferno wife."

"I wouldn't want to be anything else." She dropped her head to his shoulder. "I just have two questions."

"Name them."

"Why didn't you come home last night?"

"Because I would have wanted to prove to you once and for all that I love you, and that The Inferno exists. But I realized it was more important that you discover that for yourself. I needed you to trust me without the words. To trust your feelings for me."

"To trust in The Inferno."

"Yes." He smoothed her hair back from her face. "What's your second question?"

"What took so long?" she asked with a sigh.

He chuckled, the sound low and intimate. "I believe that's my question for you. What took you so long to trust in The Inferno?"

She answered readily enough. "The Inferno wasn't logical. It still isn't. But—" she blew out her breath "—you can't argue with facts."

He blinked in surprise, then gave a shout of laughter. "Do you realize you just called The Inferno fact?"

She wrinkled her nose. "Scary, isn't it? But that wasn't actually my second question. What I want to know is, why did it take so long to start Britt's experiment?"

"Oh, that. My brothers weren't happy about Britt changing the rules at the last minute. When she stuck Lazz and Nicolò in front of you, we almost had a riot on our hands. Even the crowd booed."

"But not you," she guessed shrewdly.

"I knew you'd find me."

Her arms tightened around him. "And now that I have, I'm never going to let you go."

Epilogue

It was a full week later before Caitlyn remembered something else she'd found in that cursed box of personal files. The instant she did, she tracked down her husband, barging straight into his office. "Marco, there's something you need to know. Something important." She offered an apologetic look. "I would have told you sooner, but—"

He lifted an eyebrow, amusement gleaming in his eyes. "You've been a little distracted?"

How could she not after the blissful week they'd shared? "Yes." She worried at her bottom lip until he put a stop to it with a lingering kiss.

"First, before we deal with any more business, I have a present for you." He held out a box that he'd personally wrapped and tied with a slightly lopsided bow. "Fair warning. It sparkles."

"Oh, Marco. You know you don't have to buy me jewelry."

"I will be buying you jewelry," he told her quite definitely. "In fact, I intend to shower you in fire diamonds. But this… This is something a little different."

Without another word, she took the box. The weight of it surprised her and she opened it, lifting out the velvet inner box. After she removed the lid, she stared at the contents and then began to laugh. He'd bought her a gorgeous glass paperweight. And floating inside the glass, like glittering diamond bubbles, was every last piece of Dante jewelry that Britt Jones had owned. She threw her arms around her husband and kissed him. How had she gotten so fortunate? A man who could make her laugh…and shower her with diamonds.

She didn't want this moment to end. And even though she knew she had endless moments like this ahead of her, soon she'd have to put romance aside and get down to business. Marco must have sensed her thoughts. He pulled back and cupped her face.

"What's wrong?" he asked.

He didn't give her a chance to respond, but took her mouth in a series of deep, penetrating kisses. It was just as well. She really didn't want to tell him that she'd found evidence in the "box from hell" that the Dantes might not be the only legal owners of the fire diamond mine.

Later. She'd tell him later about the O'Dell brothers, who were the original owners of the mine. And she'd tell him about the possibility that Cameron O'Dell's granddaughter, Kiley, could have a legitimate claim to half the mine. Or maybe she'd put Nicolò on the case. After all, he was the Dante family troubleshooter, not Marco.

Her husband pulled back again, his smile one of wicked promise. "Well? What's up?"

"Nothing important." Caitlyn tightened her arms around Marco's neck and lifted her face for another of his drugging kisses. "At least, nothing as important as this."

His expression softened and he captured her mouth once again, his words the last thing she heard before she tumbled into the golden future stretching before her. "Nothing will ever be as important as how much we love each other."

* * * * *

Nicolò's story is next.
Watch for Day Leclaire's new
DANTE LEGACY *book,*
DANTE'S WEDDING DECEPTION,
coming this July from Silhouette Desire.

THOROUGHBRED LEGACY
*The stakes are high when it comes to love,
horse racing, family secrets
and broken promises.*

*A new exciting Harlequin continuity series
coming soon!*
Led by New York Times *bestselling author
Elizabeth Bevarly*
FLIRTING WITH TROUBLE

Here's a preview!

THE DOOR CLOSED behind them, throwing them into darkness and leaving them utterly alone. And the next thing Daniel knew, he heard himself saying, "Marnie, I'm sorry about the way things turned out in Del Mar."

She said nothing at first, only strode across the room and stared out the window beside him. Although he couldn't see her well in the darkness—he still hadn't switched on a light...but then, neither had she—he imagined her expression was a little preoccupied, a little anxious, a little confused.

Finally, very softly, she said, "Are you?"

He nodded, then, worried she wouldn't be able to see the gesture, added, "Yeah. I am. I should have said goodbye to you."

"Yes, you should have."

Actually, he thought, there were a lot of things he should have done in Del Mar. He'd had *a lot* riding on the Pacific Classic, and even more on his entry, Little Joe, but after meeting Marnie, the Pacific Classic had been the last thing on Daniel's mind. His loss at Del Mar had pretty much ended his career before it had even begun, and he'd had to start all over again, rebuilding from nothing.

He simply had not then and did not now have room in his life for a woman as potent as Marnie Roberts. He was a horseman first and foremost. From the time he was a schoolboy, he'd known what he wanted to do with his life—be the best possible trainer he could be.

He had to make sure Marnie understood—and he understood, too—why things had ended the way they had eight years ago. He just wished he could find the words to do that. Hell, he wished he could find the *thoughts* to do that.

"You made me forget things, Marnie, things that I really needed to remember. And that scared the hell out of me. Little Joe should have won the Classic. He was by far the best horse entered in that race. But I didn't give him the attention he needed and deserved that week, because all I could think about was you. Hell, when I woke up that morning all I wanted to do was lie there and look at you, and then wake you up and make love to you again. If I hadn't left when I did—the way I did—I might still be lying there in that bed with you, thinking about nothing else."

"And would that be so terrible?" she asked.

"Of course not," he told her. "But that wasn't why I

was in Del Mar," he repeated. "I was in Del Mar to win a race. That was my job. And my work was the most important thing to me."

She said nothing for a moment, only studied his face in the darkness as if looking for the answer to a very important question. Finally she asked, "And what's the most important thing to you now, Daniel?"

Wasn't the answer to that obvious? "My work," he answered automatically.

She nodded slowly. "Of course," she said softly. "That is, after all, what you do best."

Her comment, too, puzzled him. She made it sound as if being good at what he did was a bad thing.

She bit her lip thoughtfully, her eyes fixed on his, glimmering in the scant moonlight that was filtering through the window. And damned if Daniel didn't find himself wanting to pull her into his arms and kiss her. But as much as it might have felt as if no time had passed since Del Mar, there were eight years between now and then. And eight years was a long time in the best of circumstances. For Daniel and Marnie, it was virtually a lifetime.

So Daniel turned and started for the door, then halted. He couldn't just walk away and leave things as they were, unsettled. He'd done that eight years ago and regretted it.

"It *was* good to see you again, Marnie," he said softly. And since he was being honest, he added, "I hope we see each other again."

She didn't say anything in response, only stood silhouetted against the window with her arms wrapped around her in a way that made him wonder whether she was doing it because she was cold, or if she just needed something—someone—to hold on to. In either case, Daniel understood. There was an emptiness clinging to him that he suspected would be there for a long time.

* * * * *

THOROUGHBRED LEGACY

coming soon wherever books are sold!

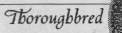

Thoroughbred *Legacy*

Launching in June 2008

A dramatic new 12-book continuity that embodies the American Dream.

Meet the Prestons, owners of Quest Stables, a successful horse-racing and breeding empire. But the lives, loves and reputations of this hardworking family are put at risk when a breeding scandal unfolds.

Flirting with Trouble

by *New York Times* bestselling author

ELIZABETH BEVARLY

Eight years ago, publicist Marnie Roberts spent seven days of bliss with Australian horse trainer Daniel Whittleson. But just as quickly, he disappeared. Now Marnie is heading to Australia to finally confront the man she's never been able to forget.

The stakes are high when it comes to love, horse racing, family secrets and broken promises.

A new exciting Harlequin continuity series coming soon!

Cole's Red-Hot Pursuit

Cole Westmoreland is a man who gets what he wants. And he wants independent and sultry Patrina Forman! She resists him—until a Montana blizzard traps them together. For three delicious nights, Cole indulges Patrina with his brand of seduction. When the sun comes out, Cole and Patrina are left to wonder—will this be the end of the passion that storms between them?

Look for

COLE'S RED-HOT PURSUIT

by USA TODAY bestselling author

BRENDA JACKSON

Available in June 2008 wherever you buy books.

Always Powerful, Passionate and Provocative.

REQUEST YOUR FREE BOOKS!

2 FREE NOVELS
PLUS 2
FREE GIFTS!

Passionate, Powerful, Provocative!

YES! Please send me 2 FREE Silhouette Desire® novels and my 2 FREE gifts (gifts are worth about $10). After receiving them, if I don't wish to receive any more books, I can return the shipping statement marked "cancel". If I don't cancel, I will receive 6 brand-new novels every month and be billed just $4.05 per book in the U.S. or $4.74 per book in Canada, plus 25¢ shipping and handling per book and applicable taxes, if any*. That's a savings of almost 15% off the cover price! I understand that accepting the 2 free books and gifts places me under no obligation to buy anything. I can always return a shipment and cancel at any time. Even if I never buy another book, the two free books and gifts are mine to keep forever.   225 SDN ERVX 326 SDN ERVM

Name	(PLEASE PRINT)

Address	Apt. #

City	State/Prov.	Zip/Postal Code

Signature (if under 18, a parent or guardian must sign)

Mail to the Silhouette Reader Service:
IN U.S.A.: P.O. Box 1867, Buffalo, NY 14240-1867
IN CANADA: P.O. Box 609, Fort Erie, Ontario L2A 5X3

Not valid to current subscribers of Silhouette Desire books.

Want to try two free books from another line?
Call 1-800-873-8635 or visit www.morefreebooks.com.

* Terms and prices subject to change without notice. N.Y. residents add applicable sales tax. Canadian residents will be charged applicable provincial taxes and GST. Offer not valid in Quebec. This offer is limited to one order per household. All orders subject to approval. Credit or debit balances in a customer's account(s) may be offset by any other outstanding balance owed by or to the customer. Please allow 4 to 6 weeks for delivery. Offer available while quantities last.

Your Privacy: Silhouette Books is committed to protecting your privacy. Our Privacy Policy is available online at www.eHarlequin.com or upon request from the Reader Service. From time to time we make our lists of customers available to reputable third parties who may have a product or service of interest to you. If you would prefer we not share your name and address, please check here. ☐

SDES08R

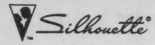

Romantic
SUSPENSE

Sparked by Danger, Fueled by Passion.

Seduction Summer:
Seduction in the sand...and a killer on the beach.

Silhouette Romantic Suspense invites you to the hottest summer yet with three connected stories from some of our steamiest storytellers! Get ready for...

Killer Temptation
by Nina Bruhns;
a millionaire this tempting is worth a little danger.

Killer Passion
by Sheri WhiteFeather;
an FBI profiler's forbidden passion incites a killer's rage,

and

Killer Affair
by Cindy Dees;
this affair with a mystery man is to die for.

Look for

KILLER TEMPTATION by Nina Bruhns in June 2008
KILLER PASSION by Sheri WhiteFeather in July 2008
and
KILLER AFFAIR by Cindy Dees in August 2008.

Available wherever you buy books!

Royal Seductions

Michelle Celmer delivers a powerful miniseries in
Royal Seductions; where two brothers fight for the
crown and discover love. In *The King's Convenient Bride*,
the king discovers his marriage of convenience to the
woman he's been promised to wed is turning all too
real. The playboy prince proposes a mock engagement
to defuse rumors circulating about him and restore
order to the kingdom...until his pretend fiancée
becomes pregnant in *The Illegitimate Prince's Baby*.

Look for

THE KING'S CONVENIENT BRIDE
&
THE ILLEGITIMATE PRINCE'S BABY

BY MICHELLE CELMER

Available in June 2008 wherever you buy books.

Always Powerful, Passionate and Provocative.

COMING NEXT MONTH

#1873 JEALOUSY & A JEWELLED PROPOSITION—
Yvonne Lindsay
Diamonds Down Under
Determined to avenge his family's name, this billionaire sets out
to take over his biggest competition...and realizes his ex may be
the perfect weapon for revenge.

#1874 COLE'S RED-HOT PURSUIT—Brenda Jackson
After a night of passion, a wealthy sheriff will stop at nothing to
get the woman back into his bed. And he always gets what he wants.

#1875 SEDUCED BY THE ENEMY—Sara Orwig
Platinum Grooms
He has a score to settle with his biggest business rival. Seducing
his enemy's daughter proves to be the perfect way to have his
revenge.

#1876 THE KING'S CONVENIENT BRIDE—
Michelle Celmer
Royal Seductions
An arranged marriage turns all too real when the king falls for his
convenient wife. Don't miss the second book in the series, also
available this June!

#1877 THE ILLEGITIMATE PRINCE'S BABY—
Michelle Celmer
Royal Seductions
The playboy prince proposes a mock engagement...until his
pretend fiancée becomes pregnant! Don't miss the first book in
this series, also on sale this June!

#1878 RICH MAN'S FAKE FIANCÉE—Catherine Mann
The Landis Brothers
Caught in a web of tabloid lies, their only recourse is a fake
engagement. But the passion they feel for one another is all
too real.

SDCNM0508